The Pony Rider Boys In The Ozarks

Frank Gee Patchin

The Pony Rider Boys in the Ozarks

Frank Gee Patchin

PO Box 2211
Fairfield, IA 52556
www.1stworldlibrary.org
First Edition

LCCN: 2005906474

Softcover ISBN: 1-4218-1530-3
Hardcover ISBN: 1-4218-1430-7
eBook ISBN: 1-4218-1630-X

The Pony Rider Boys in the Ozarks

contributed by Tim, Ed & Rodney

in support of

1st World Library Literary Society

CONTENTS

CHAPTER I

A MYSTERIOUS VISITOR

"Boys! B-o-y-s!"

There was no response to the imperative summons.

Professor Zepplin sat up in his cot, listening intently. Something had awakened him suddenly, but just what he was unable to decide.

"Be quiet over there, young men," he admonished, adding in a lower tone, "I'm sure I heard some one moving about."

The camp of the Pony Rider Boys lay wrapped in darkness, the camp-fire having long since died out. Not a sound disturbed the stillness of the night save the soft murmurings of the foliage, stirred in a gentle breeze that was drifting in from the southwest.

The Professor climbed from his cot, and, without waiting to draw on his clothes, stepped outside. He stood listening in front of his tent for several minutes, but heard nothing of a disturbing nature.

"I believe those young rascals are up to some of their pranks - either that, or I have been having bad dreams.

While I'm up I might as well make sure," he decided, tip-toeing to the tent occupied by Tad Butler and Walter Perkins.

Both were apparently sleeping soundly, while in an adjoining tent Ned Rector and Stacy Brown were breathing regularly, sleeping the sleep that naturally comes after a day in the saddle over the rugged, uneven slopes of the Ozark Mountains.

Professor Zepplin uttered something that sounded not unlike an Indian's grunt of disgust.

"Dreams!" he decided sharply. "I should not have eaten that pie last night. Pie doesn't seem to trouble those boys in the least, but it certainly has a bad effect on my digestive apparatus."

Having thus delivered himself of his opinion on the value of pie as a bedtime food, the scientist trotted back to his tent, his teeth chattering and shoulders shrugging, for the mountain air was chill and the Professor was clad only in his pajamas.

No sooner had he settled himself between his comforting blankets, however, than he suddenly started up again with a muttered exclamation.

"I knew it! I told you so!"

This time there could be no doubt. He plainly heard a dry twig snap near by; whether it were under the weight of man or beast, he did not know.

"There is something out there. It couldn't have been the pie after all. I'm going to find out what it is before I get back into this bed again," he decided firmly, slipping quietly from under the covers and peering out through the half closed flap of his tent.

As before, all was silence, the drowsy, indistinct voices of the night passing almost without notice.

But Professor Zepplin instead of waiting where he was, reached for his revolver and then strode boldly out into the open space in front of the tents, determined to solve the mystery, and, if possible, without waking the boys.

The reader no doubt already has recognized in the four boys sleeping in the little weather-beaten tents the same lads who some time before had started off for a vacation in the mountains where they hunted the cougar and the bobcat, the thrilling adventures met with on that journey having been related in a former volume entitled, "THE PONY RIDER BOYS IN THE ROCKIES."

They will be remembered, too, as the lads who, in "THE PONY RIDER BOYS IN TEXAS," crossed the plains on a cattle drive, during the course of which Tad Butler bravely saved the life of the Chinese cook, by plunging into a swollen torrent; and later, saved a large part of the great herd, himself being nearly trampled to death in a wild stampede of the cattle.

It will be recalled also, how Tad Butler and his companions, after many strange and startling experiences, solved the veiled riddle of the plains and laid the ghost of the old church of San Miguel, for all time.

The stirring adventures of "THE PONY RIDER BOYS IN MONTANA," too, are still fresh in the minds of those who have followed the fortunes of the four lads since they first started out on their journeyings.

It will he recalled that in the latter story the lads experienced the thrill of being in a real battle between the cowboys and the sheep herders on the free-grass range of the north; how Tad Butler was captured by the Blackfeet Indians, and how, with the help of an Indian maiden, he managed to make his escape.

It will also be remembered that Tad was able to rescue another lad who, like himself, had been taken by the Blackfeet, and to return the boy to his father, none the worse for his exciting experiences. It will be recalled as well, how Tad Butler through his own efforts solved the mystery of the old Custer trail - a mystery that had perplexed and annoyed the ranchers along the historic trail for many months.

And now they were once more in the saddle, having chosen the Ozark Mountains in southwestern Missouri as the scene of their next explorations.

With them they carried a pack train of four mules, these being best adapted to packing the boys' belongings over the rugged mountains. For their guide they had engaged a full-blooded Shawnee Indian named Joe Hawk, known among his people as Eagle-eye, making a party of six, with eight head of stock in all.

At the time of the beginning of this narrative the Pony Riders were encamped on a fork of the White River some three days out from Springfield. Joe Hawk had asked permission to leave the party for the night to pay a visit to a fellow-tribesman who lived somewhere in the mountains to the west of them.

On second thought it occurred to Professor Zepplin that perhaps it might have been Joe, or Eagle-eye, as the boys had decided to call the Indian, whom he had heard skulking about the camp.

"Eagle-eye," he called softly.

There was no response, so the Professor, gripping his gun resolutely, crept along toward the opposite side of the camp where the noise had seemed to come from. So quietly had he moved that he made scarcely a sound, until suddenly there came a commotion that more than made up for the noise he had so successfully avoided before.

Stacy Brown, with his usual forgetfulness, had left his saddle in the middle of the camp. The Professor caught his toe on the obstruction, measuring his length on the ground instantly, where he floundered about for a few seconds.

"Instead of discovering the other fellow, I think I am discovering myself," he growled, scrambling to his feet, gingerly rubbing a knee.

Now the Professor walked with a distinct limp, while his bare feet seemed to pick up every sharp pebble in camp, all of which added to his discomfort.

"I'd make a nice sort of scout," he muttered. "Everybody within a mile of me would know I was coming even before I got started, I guess -"

The Professor suddenly cut short his words, and

crouched down close to the ground. He thought he heard something ahead and a little to the right of him.

"Who's there?" he demanded.

No answer being made to his inquiry, he gripped his gun more firmly and crawled cautiously toward the spot where he thought he had heard some one moving. The night was so dark that he could make nothing out of the shadows about him, being obliged therefore to trust entirely to his sense of hearing.

Now he was certain that some one was in camp who had no business there, for the sound of footsteps was plainly borne to his ears - cautious, catlike steps, as if the intruder were seeking to get away without attracting attention.

The Professor, determined to capture the intruder, getting down on all fours to avoid possible detection, made a wide detour so as to come up behind where the fellow seemed to be at that moment. After much labor he managed to reach the desired position.

The Professor straightened up to listen. He must be close upon the other by this time. But what was his chagrin to hear those same footsteps on the opposite side of the camp. Professor Zepplin by much effort had just come from the other side himself.

"Stupid!" he muttered. "I'll take no roundabout way this time. I'll go straight ahead and be as quiet about it as I can."

He did so. He moved straight across the camp ground, not forgetting the saddle which he carefully avoided, but narrowly missing falling over it a second time.

By the time he had crossed to his former position, the intruder had done likewise. Professor Zepplin dodged behind a tree.

By this time the scientist was beginning to feel a little worried. He could not understand what the other fellow's object might be. If it were robbery, the fellow certainly would desire to get away as quickly as possible, rather than remain when he knew that efforts were being made to capture him. If not plunder, what could be his purpose?

With suddenly formed determination, Professor Zepplin strode out from his hiding place, starting for the other side on a run.

The other man did the same, and the only result of the move was that their positions were exchanged.

Once more the Professor decided to try strategy and see if he could not come up behind his opponent.

At the same moment the visitor apparently decided to resort to the same tactics. They went in opposite directions, however, to carry out their purpose, and when each arrived at the place it was to find that the other was opposite him again.

The Professor's bare feet were in a sad state by this time, his pajamas were torn and his hands were worn tender from using them for feet when running along on all fours. At the same time his temper was wearing to a point of dangerous thinness. It was likely to break down the slender barrier that held it at almost any time.

Suddenly he realized that the intruder had been silent for some minutes, and the Professor decided that it was time he ceased thinking over his own troubles and paid more attention to what the other man was doing.

"Now, I wonder what he is up to," growled the scientist. "I believe he has given me the slip and gotten away. Here I've been dreaming for minutes. I'll slip some myself and see if I can't surprise him if he's there yet."

Once again he started across the camp ground, without resorting to any of his former tactics, other than to proceed with extreme caution, covering the intervening space with long, careful strides.

Reaching the rock, he paused to listen, but could hear nothing.

Gun ready for instant use, Professor Zepplin dashed around the corner of the rock, running plump into the arms of the fellow whom he had been so successfully dodging for the past twenty minutes.

So startled was the scientist that he dropped his revolver, throwing both arms about his antagonist. He was surprised at the slenderness of the fellow, though he quickly discovered that what the other lacked in bulk he easily made up for by his lithe, supple body and muscular arms.

Almost before Professor Zepplin had collected his wits sufficiently to make any sort of defense he found himself lying flat on his back, with his opponent sitting on top of him, both wrists pinioned to the ground in an iron grip.

There seemed to the Professor something strangely familiar about the figure that was holding him down so firmly, but he did not try to analyze the impression. He had other things to think of at that moment.

"I'll wait a second until he lets up ever so little, then, with my superior weight, I ought to be able to throw him -"

"I've got you this time. What do you mean by prowling about our camp at this time of the -"

"Wha - what - who - who - " exclaimed the Professor.

"What!" fairly shouted the other. "Who - who are you?"

"I'm Professor Zepplin. Who are you?"

"Oh, shucks! I'm Tad Butler," answered the boy, hastily releasing his prisoner, and, more crestfallen than he would have cared to admit, assisting the Professor to his feet.

"What do you mean, you young rascal?" demanded the Professor, grasping the boy by the shoulders and shaking him vigorously. "I say, what do you mean by playing such pranks on me as this? Why, I might have shot you. I -"

"You are wrong, Professor; I have not intentionally played pranks on you -"

"Yes you have - yes you have," fumed the Professor.

"I might accuse you of doing the same thing to me,

only I know you didn't get up in the middle of the night to play hide and seek with a boy -"

"Then what does this mean? Answer me instantly!"

"I can do so easily. The fact is, I heard somebody prowling around. The slight noise awakened me -"

"I should think it might," snarled Professor Zepplin.

"And, without waiting to dress, I slipped out -"

"And led me a nice chase. Look at me. There isn't a spot on my body that isn't black and blue. And to think I've been running around here in my bare feet trying to catch you -"

"You haven't entirely. You were chasing the same thing that I was," answered Tad thoughtfully.

"What's that? What's that you say?"

"I mean that somebody was here - somebody who had no business to be here."

"You mean -"

"Yes, I mean that after I had been out here a few moments I distinctly heard two men. One of them, it appears, was yourself. Who the other was I don't know. He evidently got away. As I couldn't follow both of them, I chose you. You seemed to be the easiest one to catch. I was right, wasn't I?" laughed the boy, at the thought of the game they had been playing with each other.

"Somebody else here? I knew it, I knew it," exclaimed the Professor. "When I first came out you were sound asleep. I must have awakened you when I fell over the saddle out there. Who left that thing there for me to nearly break my neck on?" he demanded angrily.

"I guess it must be Chunky's saddle."

"Of course. I'll talk to him in the morning. I'm going to bed. I'll catch my death of cold."

CHAPTER II

A PACK MULE GOES OVER A CLIFF

Next morning the boys, assisted by Eagle-eye, had prepared the breakfast by the time the Professor had awakened. They took keen satisfaction in calling him for breakfast. Ordinarily they slept so late that the Professor had to turn them out by physical force.

"Anybody'd think you'd been keeping late hours, Professor," laughed Ned Rector.

"Perhaps I have," answered the scientist good naturedly. "But if so, I am not the only one of this party who has."

That the Professor's words held some meaning unknown to them the boys were fully aware. Tad had said nothing of his experiences of the previous night, so they did not think to turn to him for an explanation.

"I might as well tell you, young gentlemen, that there was some one prowling about this camp after we all were asleep last night -"

"What!" cried the Pony Riders in sudden surprise.

"Yes, that is true. Thaddeus and myself chased him

around for nearly half an hour, but -"

All eyes were now turned on Tad, who was bending over his plate that they might not observe the grin that was spreading over his face despite the lad's effort to keep it down.

"O Tad, tell us all about it," urged Walter Perkins. "What was he, a bold robber or what?"

"I guess he must have been an 'Or What,'" suggested Stacy Brown wisely.

"Don't mind him. He's dreaming still. It's only his appetite that's here at the table. The rest of him is in bed asleep," jeered Ned Rector, with such a funny grimace that the boys laughed.

"Yes," answered Tad, looking up, "we ran around here in our pajamas until we found each other. Then we gave it up and went to bed."

"But who was it?" insisted Walter.

"It was an -"

"Now, never mind, Chunky. You are supposed to be asleep," admonished Ned, with a superior wave of his hand.

"I cannot say as to that," answered Tad. "I really don't think it amounted to so very much. Probably some prowler curious to know what sort of camp he had stumbled upon. I didn't lose any sleep over it after I got back to bed."

"Neither did Chunky," laughed Ned.

"Did you?" asked the fat boy sharply, turning the laugh on Ned.

"You remember what we were told in Springfield," said Walter.

"What was that?" asked the Professor.

"That a band of robbers had been causing considerable excitement in the Ozarks for several months past."

"Yes, you are right. I had forgotten that," nodded Professor Zepplin. "Stealing horses and other things."

"Yes."

"But it's all nonsense to think they would bother us," objected Ned. "We haven't anything that they would want."

"No, nor do we want them," replied Walter, with emphasis. "I guess we had better sleep on our rifles to-night."

"That will hardly be necessary," smiled the Professor.

"How about Eagle-eye?" asked Ned. "Didn't he hear anything?"

"Eagle-eye was away last night."

"Oh, yes, that's so. I had forgotten that."

"It might be a good idea to tell him about it," suggested

Tad, glancing over at the Professor.

Professor Zepplin nodded his head.

"Eagle-eye, will you come here, please?" called Tad.

The Shawnee, who had been pottering about the camp-fire, strode over to them with his almost noiseless tread, and squatted on the ground near the breakfast table.

"There was somebody here last night, Eagle-eye," Tad informed him in an impressive voice.

The Shawnee nodded.

"Of course, you not having been here, you knew nothing about it, but to-night you'd better sleep with one eye open.

"Joe Hawk know," answered the Indian.

"Know what?" demanded the Professor sharply.

"Know Indian come last night," was the startling announcement.

"What's that? What's that, Eagle-eye? You mean yourself, I presume. You mean you came back. But that is not the point -"

The Indian shook his head with emphasis.

"Other Indian come."

Tad nodded at his companions as if to say, "I told

you so."

Then the Shawnee did know more than he had seen fit to tell them?

"Tell us about it, Eagle-eye."

"Joe Hawk find trail of canoe on river at sun-up," answered the Indian tersely.

"A trail on the river?" demanded Stacy, suddenly breaking into uproarious laughter, which died away in an indistinct gurgle when he found the eyes of his companions fixed sternly upon him. "Funny place to find a trail," he muttered, threatening to indulge in another fit of merriment.

"I don't understand you, Eagle-eye," said the Professor. "You say you found the trail of a canoe on the river?"

"Yes."

"That sounds peculiar. I agree with Master Stacy that it is a most remarkable place to find a trail hours after. Perhaps you will explain."

Eagle-eye rose to his feet.

"Come. I show you."

All rose from the table, forgetful that they were eating their breakfast, and followed the guide down the steep bank to the river.

"There trail," he announced, pointing a long, bronzed finger at the edge of the water.

Tad stooped over, examining the shore critically.

"The Shawnee is right," he said, turning to the Professor.

"How do you know? What have you found?"

"There. You can see for yourself. It is distinctly marked -"

"What's marked?" demanded Stacy, pressing forward.

"You can see where the keel of a canoe has rested in the dirt there. The trail is ever so faint, but it is unmistakably there. See how it broadens out as it extends backward until it reaches the gravel in the stream."

"Moccasin tracks," grunted the guide.

"Where?" asked Walter, apprehensively.

"There," answered the Indian, pointing up the bank whence they had just come.

The boys looked at each other in wondering silence.

"What do you think is the meaning of the visit, Eagle-eye?" asked the Professor.

The Shawnee shrugged his shoulders.

"Mebby hungry."

"That is a sensible explanation of the visit," decided Professor Zepplin. "What other motive could an Indian have for a visit at that hour? There is no cause for alarm. But I wish if any more hungry ones pay us a visit, they would do so in the day time, so as not to interrupt my sleep."

"And mine," laughed Tad.

"Yah-hum," yawned Stacy, sleepily.

"I told you you weren't awake yet," growled Ned. "Let's all go back to our breakfast."

"I second the motion," laughed the Professor. "We are forgetting all about the inner man. And it is time we were getting on our way if we are to make any great progress to-day."

Anxious to be in the saddle again, the boys bounded up the bank and hastily finished their breakfast. While they were doing so the guide stoically busied himself with packing the cooking kits and loading the pack mules, so that by the time the lads were ready all save their own belongings had been stowed away.

It was the work of a few minutes only to strike their tents, fold blankets and pack their personal belongings. They had now been roughing it long enough so that they had become really expert in the work. And, besides, they had learned to get together a fairly satisfying meal out of not much of anything. They had learned many other things that were to prove useful to them in after years, but which at the time was making little or no impression upon them.

Fairly radiating health and spirits, the boys threw themselves into their saddles with a shout. The guide led the way, leading the mule train, and his pace was so rapid that the pack animals were put to their best to keep up with him. Most of the time he appeared to be dragging the led mule, instead of leading it.

"A wonderful country," breathed the Professor, as they finally came out on a high elevation that gave them a glimpse of the eastern slope of the mountains.

They halted to take in the magnificent view.

"This is what is known as the 'Ozark Uplift,'" the Professor informed them.

"I should call it a downfall," answered Ned, gazing off at the deep gorges and jagged precipices. "Why do you call it that?"

The Professor waxed eloquent.

"From the earliest time, young gentlemen, this region has been subject to uprising or downsinking. In all sections of its area it has experienced the effects of powerful dynamic forces -"

"Dynamite - did they use dynamite to blow the mountains up into such shapes as that?" asked Stacy innocently.

"I said nothing about dynamite. Dynamic was the word I used," replied Professor Zepplin, casting a withering glance at the fat boy.

"Oh," Stacy exclaimed.

"It is therefore called the 'Ozark Uplift.'"

"That is interesting," answered Ned solemnly, though it is doubtful if he understood what the Professor was really talking about.

"There is still another of tremendous import connected with this region. You will all be interested in it," announced the Professor impressively.

The boys gathered about him in a circle, meantime allowing their ponies to nibble at the green leaves.

"Yes," urged Tad.

"The region where is now located the Ozark Uplift is said to have been the first land to appear above the waters of the continental ocean."

"You - you mean -" stammered Ned.

"He means this was the first land to appear above the water when this continent was all an ocean," spoke up Tad, with quick understanding.

Stacy urged his pony further into the circle. His face was flushed and he evidently was filled with some sudden new thought.

"What is it, Master Stacy?" asked the Professor.

"You - you say this was the first land to -"

"Yes, so it has been said."

"Then - then this - then this must have been where the Ark landed," exploded the fat boy.

For a few seconds a profound silence greeted this announcement. Then the lads broke out into a shout of laughter. Even Professor Zepplin threw his head back and laughed immoderately.

"I am afraid, my young friend, that the place where the ancient craft ran aground was some distance from this rugged spot -"

"But why not?" persisted the boy.

"In the first place, this continent came to life some time after the event you speak of is supposed to have taken place."

"Oh," muttered the lad.

"And now we had better be pressing on."

"When do we reach the Red Star Mine?" asked Ned.

"You will have to ask Eagle-eye. I don't know."

The Indian, when questioned on this point, said the Red Star Mine lay three suns to the southwest of them.

The country seemed to be getting more rough as they proceeded, and it had now become necessary to move with extreme caution for fear of plunging over one of the many abrupt cliffs that now and then appeared almost under the feet of the advancing train.

But the Indian seemed to feel no concern over these. He merely changed his course, skirting the canyon until a turn in its winding course enabled him to head straight into the southwest again.

Not even in the Rockies had the boys met with such peculiar formations as now appeared on all sides of them.

"I'd hate to travel this trail in the night," growled Stacy.

"You wouldn't have to travel it far," laughed Tad. "You'd be walking on air before you knew it."

Stacy had pressed on ahead while the others were talking. He had observed what they had not. One of the pack mules had lagged behind, and with head lowered almost to the ground appeared to have gone sound asleep. The Shawnee, engaged with his own thoughts, apparently was unaware that he had left a mule behind.

The fat boy, with great glee, was urging his pony quietly along, approaching the pack animal with as much caution as possible. It was Stacy's intention to give the beast the fright of its life, in which ambition he succeeded beyond his fondest anticipations.

Getting near enough for his purpose, Stacy slipped from his pony, hunted about until he found a stick long enough for his purpose, and with this crept up on the sleeping mule.

With a shrill shriek the lad brought the stick down on the long-eared animal's rump with a whack that, while it could not have hurt, did all that he had hoped it might.

Both the mule's hind feet shot up into the air, while the beast with a short, sharp bray of fright lunged straight ahead.

The guide uttered a shrill exclamation of warning as he saw the mule tearing through the bushes to the left of the trail. Leaving his two pack animals, Eagle-eye leaped for the fleeing one.

But he was too late.

All at once the frightened beast appeared to stand on his head, his hind feet beating a tattoo in the air; then he disappeared altogether.

The Pony Rider Boys, hearing the disturbance, had hurried up, and just in time to see the final scene in the little tragedy that their companion had caused.

"What's this? What's this?" demanded the Professor. "What's the matter?"

"Pony fall down! Pony fall down!" exclaimed the Indian, with a trace of excitement in his tone.

"He means our long-eared friend has taken a header over that rock there," Ned Rector informed them.

"I am afraid it is more serious than that," added Tad. "It looked to me as if the pack mule went over a cliff."

"Him fall down, fall down, fall down," repeated the guide.

Chunky, frightened at the result of his prank, had quickly scrambled into his own saddle and drawn back from the scene of his late exploit.

Professor Zepplin did not understand how it had happened.

"I'm to blame, sir," announced Chunky, plucking up courage and riding up beside the Professor. "I hit him with a stick and he ran away."

In spite of the disaster that had come upon them, the boys could not but laugh at the boy's rueful countenance. Nor did the Professor find it in his heart to be harsh.

"You deserve to be punished, sir, but somehow when I look at you my anger vanishes instantly. The next question is, how are we going to get the beast up here? What do you say, guide?"

"Him dead."

"What's that?"

"Pack pony, him gone Happy Hunting Ground."

"You don't mean he has been killed?"

The guide nodded with emphasis, at the same time bringing the palms of his hands sharply together to convey the impression that the mule had hit the rocks below so hard that he would never rise of his own accord again.

"Now we are in a fix," said Ned.

"I guess we had better make Chunky walk and use his pony for packing the outfit," suggested Walter.

"Yes, but we have little or no outfit to pack," answered Tad. "Most of it is down there with the dead mule; how far I don't know."

The Pony Rider Boys gasped. This, indeed, was a serious situation.

CHAPTER III

A DARING PROPOSAL

For a full moment the boys looked at each other doubtfully. Professor Zepplin was the first to break the silence.

"Wha - what pack did the mule have?"

"Part of the kitchen outfit and all of the canned goods," answered Tad Butler impressively.

Ned Rector laughed.

"This is where we give our stomachs a rest," he mocked.

"I fail to see anything humorous in our present predicament," chided the Professor. "We are many miles from our base of supplies, with our supplies at the bottom of a gorge, goodness knows how deep down. Whether we can get down there or not I haven't the slightest idea -"

"Don't we get anything to eat?" wailed Chunky.

"Think you deserve to have anything?" demanded Ned.

"Don't be hard on him," spoke up Tad. "He feels cut up

enough about it as it is. We've all done just as foolish things, only they didn't happen to turn out the way this one has."

Chunky turned his pony about and rode a few paces away from them, being more disturbed than he cared to have his companions know.

"Eagle-eye," called the Professor.

The Indian was leaning over the cliff looking down into the deep canyon, trying to find the pack mule. He straightened up and strode over to the Professor upon being called.

"You sure the mule is dead?"

"Mule no pack more."

"Can you get down there to gather up our belongings?"

Eagle-eye shook his head.

"No get um."

"Why not?" interjected Walter.

"Pony fall in - Injun fall in," grunted the Shawnee.

"But can we not go forward or else back a mile or so and find an entrance to the gorge?" demanded the Professor.

"Yes, that's the idea. Of course we can," urged Ned. "We are not half as bad off as we thought. Of course the mule is done for, but we can divide up the pack amongst us boys and carry it all right until we get where we can either hire or buy another mule. Don't think a little thing like that will stop us."

"How about it, Eagle-eye?" asked Tad.

"No get um. Water him deep. Him cold, b-r-r-r! Pony drown, Indian drown. Mebby fat boy drown, too."

"That seems to settle it," announced the Professor. "We shall have to hold a council of war, as Eagle-eye does not seem to have any suggestions to make. What have you to say about it, Master Tad?"

"I think it would be a good idea to take a look over the cliff before offering any suggestions," answered the lad, dismounting and tethering his pony. "Perhaps the guide may be wrong."

One look over the bold cliff, however, was sufficient to convince Tad of the correctness of the Indian's judgment. He found himself gazing down into one of those deep canyons that had been cut through the mountains by water courses during hundreds of years.

The wall on each side, while nearly straight up and down, was jagged and broken, but so precipitous as to make any idea of descending it impossible. There was not a bush nor shrub in sight until near the bottom, where Tad discovered a thick growth of bushes on the edge of the swiftly flowing water course.

A disturbed spot among these showed where the pack mule had fallen. That he had not gone on into the stream and been swept away was due to the matted growth down there. The others had joined Tad by the time he had made up his mind that their guide had described the situation correctly.

"What do you make of it, Master Tad?" asked the Professor.

"Nothing very encouraging."

"Whew! That's a drop!" exclaimed Ned, peering cautiously over. "Where is our kitchen outfit?"

"There, where you see the bushes trampled down. What there is left of it, anyway. But perhaps the canvas wrapped around the stuff has protected it from serious damage."

"Little difference it makes to us whether or not," answered the Professor. "The supplies are lost and that's all there is about it. We have scarcely enough left to carry us through the day."

"No!" said Walter. "Then what are we going to do?"

"I don't know, Master Walter."

"We've got to get the stuff up here, that's all," answered Tad, with a firm compression of the lips.

"Then you'll have to borrow a flying machine if you do. That's the only way we'll ever reach the pack mule. Why, it's a mile down there -"

"Not quite," answered Tad.

"How deep do you think the gorge is, Tad?" asked the Professor.

"Oh, forty or fifty feet, I should say. I hardly think it is deeper than that. But that is quite enough -"

Tad, in the meantime, had been considering the problem, thinking deeply on the best means of solving it.

"Yes, I think I can do it," he decided.

"Do what?" asked Walter.

"Get the stuff up."

"How?" demanded Ned sharply.

"Why, go down after it, of course."

"Out of the question," answered the Professor, with emphasis.

"No, I think it can be done, if you will allow me to -"

"You mean, Master Ted, that you will attempt to get to the bottom of that gorge and bring up the provisions?"

"Yes, sir; I'll try it."

"Impossible. I cannot permit it."

"I should say not," growled Ned. "If anybody goes it should be the guide. He is an expert at climbing, I should imagine, and -" Tad laughed.

"Why, my dear Ned, you couldn't even push Eagle-eye down there. For some reason he seems to have a superstitious dread of that place. I don't know why, for Indians are not supposed to be much afraid of anything. I'll ask him. Eagle-eye, will you go down there and try to get the provisions for us?" asked Tad, turning to the guide.

Eagle-eye shrugged his shoulders, at the same time giving a negative twist to his body.

"Eagle-eye not go down there," he grunted.

"Why not?" asked Ned.

"Bad spirits live in waters. Bymeby come out and get Eagle-eye."

"Oh, shucks!" jeered Ned. "My opinion is that they wouldn't bother to get you, even if there were any such things down there."

"Then there remains only one thing for us to do," said the Professor.

"And that?" queried Walter.

"Get to the nearest settlement as quickly as possible."

"That would take at least a day or two, would it not?" inquired Tad.

"Yes, I believe so."

"Then why not let me try - at least make an effort to recover our things? Why, just think of the amount of stuff we are losing, Professor."

"But the risk, Tad. No, I cannot assume the responsibility -"

"I'll take the risk of all that. The only danger will be up here. I shall not be taking any risks to speak of -"

"How do you propose to go about it, young man?"

"Simplest thing imaginable. I'll climb down with a rope around me, so that in case I slip anywhere you can straighten me up. I promise you I will not fall."

"The next question is, where are you going to get the rope?"

"I have one that is plenty long enough," answered Tad.

"You mean the quarter-inch rope?" spoke up Walter. "That's in the pack that went over the cliff."

Tad Butler's face fell.

"Guess you are mistaken, Walt," corrected Ned. "You threw that rope down when you were packing. I picked it up and it's in my kit on my pony now."

"Hurrah!" shouted the other boys. "You can't down the Pony Riders."

Tad hurried to Ned's mount, and, pulling down the pack, secured the precious rope, which he adjusted about his waist carefully, the others observing him silently.

"I guess I am ready now, boys. I'll tell you what I want you to do, so pay close heed to what I am about to say."

CHAPTER IV

INTO THE CANYON

"Thaddeus, I cannot consent to this. I -"

"Please, now, Professor, don't stop me. I'm all right, don't you see I am?"

"Yes, at this precise moment you are. It's the moments to come that I am thinking about."

"Don't you worry one little bit. Walt, will you bring me two of those staking-down ropes? I want to splice them on in case this one should prove to be a little short. Distance is deceptive, looking down, as we are here."

"What do you want us to do?" asked Ned.

"Hold on to the rope, that's all."

"In other words, we are to be a sort of 'tug-of-war' team, eh? Is that it?"

"I suppose it is, Ned."

"Then I hope we win."

"I sincerely hope you do, too," laughed Tad.

"If I win, I'll lose. That sounds funny, doesn't it?"

"What do you mean?" demanded Chunky, pushing his way forward.

"He means," Walter informed him, "that if he wins it will be because he takes a tumble to the bottom of the canyon. Understand?"

"Oh," muttered Chunky, thrusting his hands into his trousers pockets. He stepped to the edge of the cliff, where he stood peering over curiously.

"I hope Tad doesn't win, too," he decided sagely, whereat the others laughed loudly.

"Now, Professor, will you please take charge of the operations?"

"Certainly. But, you understand, I permit this thing under strong protest. I am doing wrong. I should use my authority to prevent it were we not already in such a serious predicament."

"Don't worry. What I want is to have you take a few turns around that small tree there with the rope, and pay it out carefully, so that I can lower myself safely. Don't give me too much rope at one time, you know."

"No," chuckled Ned. "You know what they say happens to people who have too much rope."

"You mean?"

"That they usually hang themselves."

Tad laughed softly.

"Please call that lazy Indian over here and set him to work. Little does he care what trouble we're in. See, he's asleep against a tree now."

"Yes, his head would fall off if it were not nailed fast to him," added Ned, striding to the Shawnee and giving him a violent shake. "Wake up, you sleepy head!" shouted Ned in a voice that brought the Indian quickly to his feet.

"Come over here, Eagle-eye. You're wanted," called Walter.

"Put the Indian on the end of the rope; and, Professor, you please take a hold nearest to the tree. You'll be my salvation. The rest of you, except Chunky, can stand between the Professor and Eagle-eye."

They took their places as directed, while Tad straightened out the rope until it extended to the edge of the cliff.

"What do you want me to do? Have I got to stand here and look on?" demanded Stacy.

"No, Chunky. You may run the signal tower," laughed Tad.

"What's that? I don't see any such thing around here?"

"You are it."

"What? I'm what?" answered the fat boy, plainly puzzled.

"You are the signal tower in this case. That is, you will stand here and watch me. When I give a signal you will receive and pass it on to the others."

"What kind of signals?"

"That's what I'm trying to tell you, if you will give me the chance. When I hold up my hand, it means that they are to stop letting out rope. When I move it up and down, it means they are to let out on the rope a little. Understand?"

"Oh, yes; that's easy. When they shake their hand, it means you want to go up or down," exclaimed the lad enthusiastically.

"O Chunky, you're hopeless. No, no! Nothing of the kind. Listen. When I move my hand up and down, just like this - Understand?"

"Sure."

"That means I want to go down further. They don't wave their hands at all, at least I hope they don't while I am hanging in the air. Now, do you think you understand?"

"Yes, I understand."

"Repeat the directions to me then, please."

Stacy did so.

"That's right. See that you don't forget. Remember, I'm depending upon you, Chunky, and if you fail me, I may be killed."

"Don't you worry about me, Tad," answered Stacy, swelling with pride because of the responsibility that had been placed upon his plump shoulders. "I can make motions as well as anybody. Eagle-eye, tend to business over there. Get hold of that rope. Twist it around your arm. There, that's right."

"Hear, hear!" cried the boys.

Such self-confidence they had never observed in their companion before. And then again, they were trying to be as jolly as possible, that they might not give too much thought to the seriousness of the undertaking before them.

"Chunky's coming into his own," muttered Ned. "He'll be wanting to thrash some of us next. See if he doesn't."

"I think I am all ready now," announced Tad, casting a critical glance at the men holding the rope, then taking a careful survey of the depths below him.

He was standing on the very edge of the cliff, a position that would have made the average person dizzy. Yet it seemed to have no effect at all on Tad Butler.

He motioned for them to let out a little rope.

"More rope!" bellowed Stacy.

"All right, Captain," jeered Ned. "Better port your helm, though, or the rope will give you a side wipe and take you along over with Tad."

Stacy quickly changed his position, which Tad had intended telling him to do.

Without another word Tad sat down with his feet dangling over, then crawled cautiously down the steep wall. For a short distance he was able to do this without depending on the rope, Stacy in the meanwhile lying flat on his stomach, peering down and passing on the signals to those holding the rope.

Now Tad came to a piece of rock that was straight up and down and perfectly smooth. He motioned for them to lower him slowly, which they did until the boy's feet once more touched a solid footing.

He carefully settled down until he was in a sitting posture. He was on a narrow, shelving rock, and there he remained for a few moments to rest, for the trip thus far had been exceedingly trying.

"The water's fine, Chunky," he called up cheerfully.

"The water's fine," bellowed Chunky, glaring at his companions. Then a sheepish grin spread over his countenance when he realized what he had said. "I mean, that's what Tad called," he explained, amid a roar of laughter.

"He won't find it so fine if he falls in," muttered Walter.

"Bad spirits in water," grunted the Indian.

"Unfortunately for us, they're not all down there," growled Ned. But his barbed wit failed to penetrate the tough skin of the red man.

"Tend to business, boys," warned the Professor, observing a series of frantic gestures on the part of Stacy Brown. "What does he want, to be lowered?"

"Yes, yes, don't you understand?"

"No, we don't understand motions in a foreign language," laughed Walter, permitting the rope to slip through his hands a little.

"How's that?" queried Professor Zepplin.

"More rope!" roared Stacy. "Watch my signals, then you'll know what to do."

"What not to do," muttered Ned.

Once more Tad began his cautious creeping down the uncertain trail. Though he had gone some distance, it seemed to him as if the bottom were further away than when he started.

"I'm afraid this rope is not going to be long enough," he breathed. "However, I believe I can crawl down the last fifteen or twenty feet if the line will only reach to them. It's not nearly so steep down there as it is higher up."

There occurred a sudden sharp jolt on the rope, due to the men above not letting the loops slip around the tree while the rope was taut. This gave Tad a drop of three or four feet and a jar that made him think he was falling.

"Here you, up there! What are you trying to do?"

"What do you fellows mean?" demanded Stacy.

"Just a slip, that's all," answered Walter.

"Somebody slipped," shouted Stacy.

"Tell them to be careful, Chunky. This rope won't stand many such jerks as that. Remember, it's running over some sharp rocks above here and is liable to be cut in two."

Stacy transmitted the order in a loud tone of command, which the Professor emphasized by a sharp command to the boys, at the same time admitting that he himself had also been at fault.

"Tell him we will not make that mistake again, Chunky," said the Professor.

"Won't do it again," called Stacy, passing the word along.

"All right. I'm doing well now. Just keep the line fairly steady so that I won't lose my footing."

He was obliged to raise his voice now, being a long way down the slope, with the goal still far from him.

"Who would have ever thought it so far?" Tad asked himself. "I'm sure now that the rope will not reach."

Believing that he could obtain a better footing a little to the right of him, he motioned for more rope, then raised his hand aloft as a signal that he had sufficient for present needs, all of which Stacy repeated with more or less correctness.

Tad had gained a broad, shelving rock this time. Above him projected a rocky roof that reminded him of the roof over his mother's porch at home. It shut off his view of the cliff above him entirely. Straight down below him roared the river, here and there a spout of white spray shooting up into the air, revealing the presence of a hidden, treacherous rock.

It was an impressive moment for Tad Butler up there alone, with nothing between himself and sudden death save a slender quarter-inch strand of rope.

But though he felt the loneliness of his position, he felt no fear; he was impressed with the solitary grandeur of it all. Time was pressing, however, and he decided that he must continue his descent.

Stepping back to his former position, he started to grope his way downward. For several minutes he made more rapid headway than he had at any time before.

He was congratulating himself that he would soon be at the bottom of the cliff, which lay about twenty feet below him.

All at once he gave a gasp as he felt the rock crumble beneath his feet. He had thrown his weight on a piece of crumbling limestone and it had given way.

At that moment he had some two or three feet of slack rope, that he had motioned to them to pay out, as the way was not now nearly so steep.

Grasping wildly for some projecting rock to break the jolt which he knew would come when he reached the end of his rope, and perhaps seriously hurt him, the boy was able to stay his progress a little.

However, the pressure that his body threw on the slender rope was so great as to jolt nearly all the air from his lungs.

Then Tad suddenly made another and terrifying discovery.

He was going down. He was falling.

At the top of the cliff another scene was being enacted. The sudden jolt on the rope had occurred just after the boys had paid out the rope beyond the place where Tad had spliced it before beginning his descent.

The strain was too great for it. The ropes parted at a weak spot near the knot.

The Pony Riders were too much stunned to do more than gaze upon that which they believed meant the death of their companion.

Chunky, who appeared to be the coolest of any, had been watching the knot approaching him with almost fascinated interest. He was speculating what would happen should the knot chance to come apart. And the very emergency that he was considering did happen.

"The rope's broken!" shouted the Professor.

But Chunky had no need to be told that. He knew it already, almost before they realized it.

With great presence of mind, and an agility that none would have given him credit for, the fat boy threw himself upon the line that was whisking over the cliff.

Somehow he managed to fasten both hands on it.

The boy began to slide along the ground with the speed of an express train.

"Grab him! Grab him, somebody! He's going over the cliff!"

"Let go!" bellowed Ned Rector.

Stacy hung on grimly, perhaps not realizing the danger he was in. At any rate, he was determined to save Tad if he could.

"There he goes!" fairly screamed the Professor.

Chunky slipped over the brink and disappeared with a terrified "Wow!"

"They're both down there, now," groaned the Professor, leaning against the tree and wiping the perspiration from his brow.

CHAPTER V

RESCUED BY A HUMAN CHAIN

Too much stupefied to speak, even to move, the other two boys stood pale and trembling. There was no doubt in their minds that both Tad and Stacy had been killed.

"Do something! Do something!" shouted the Professor, recovering his voice in a sudden rush of words.

"I - I am afraid there is nothing we can do now," stammered Walter.

But Ned Rector had bounded to the edge and was gazing over half fearfully.

"There's Chunky! There he is!" he shouted.

"Where? Where?" cried the Professor, running up. "Where is he, I say?"

"Right down there, not more than ten feet below us. He has lodged between two rocks - no, I see now, he's caught on one."

Now that they looked closer, they observed that he was hanging head down, doubled over like a sack of meal, a sharp rock having caught in his left trousers pocket, thus stopping his downward flight.

It was not a very secure position at best.

"Are you hurt, Chunky?" called Walter.

"I - I don't know. I think I'm killed."

"Can you see Tad? Do you know what happened to him?" asked Ned, in an excited tone.

"No, I can't. I've got troubles of my own. Get me out of here quick. I can't hold on much longer."

"If the trousers only hold out, we'll save you," cried Walter. "Get a rope, Eagle-eye."

"Move! Move, idiot!" snorted the Professor. "What are you standing there for?"

Eagle-eye shrugged his shoulders, if anything more indifferently than before.

"No rope," he answered, as if it were a matter of no moment.

"I'll get a lariat. That surely ought to be long enough," said Walter, darting away to the ponies.

"Come back. There's no lariats there. They're all in the pack down at the bottom of the canyon," shouted Ned.

"Then we're helpless," groaned the Professor.

"No, we're not. I'll find a way to get the boy out,"

announced Ned, in a voice of stern determination. There was no laughter in his face now. Purpose was written in every line of it.

"Come here, you lazy redskin, you," he commanded, which summons Eagle-eye obeyed reluctantly.

"What are you going to do?" demanded the Professor.

"Help!" came a wail from the unhappy Chunky.

"We're coming. Keep quiet. Don't you move," admonished Walter.

"I'll get a nosebleed if I have to hang here this way."

"You'll get worse than that if you don't get a grip on yourself and keep quiet. I'm going to form a human chain, the way we used to do to get pond lilies at home. Professor, lie down there, while I tie your feet to the tree. We will use you for an anchor."

In a trice the Professor's feet were made fast to the tree with the remaining piece of rope that had broken off short.

"Down on your stomach, Eagle-eye!" commanded the resourceful Ned, giving the redskin a jerk that sent him sprawling. "Take hold of his ankles and hang on, Professor. You next, Walter. Good. Now grab me by the ankles, while I go over head first."

But Ned's carefully laid plans failed. The human chain was not long enough to reach.

"Pull back, quick!" he ordered.

The return, however, was less easily executed, and perspiring, weak and trembling, Ned finally succeeded in scrambling to the cliff, with the aid of those behind him.

"What can we do now?" begged the Professor, greatly agitated.

"Try it another way, that's all. We've simply got to do it. Sit down and brace your feet against that boulder near the edge, there, Professor."

This Professor Zepplin did quickly. Walter dropped down in front of him, and next came the Shawnee and Ned Rector, each, save the Professor, sitting on his knees, facing the edge of the cliff.

"Now each one grab the ankles of the one ahead of him," directed Ned.

As they did so, the sitting men and boys, still doubled up, let themselves fall forward on their faces.

Slowly the line lengthened out like the unwinding of the coils of a serpent, Ned Rector slipping slowly over the brink, the red man squirming after him, until both were clear of the edge, hanging head down.

"I've got him," came up the muffled voice of Ned. "But I've got a rush of blood to the head. Pull now! Pull for all you're worth, all of you. If you slip we're all gone. Be careful."

His words of caution were not needed. Each realized the responsibility that rested upon his shoulders, and each was bending every nerve and muscle in his body to the task.

Eagle-eye himself was urged to renewed efforts by the certain knowledge that if he failed he would go to join the "evil spirits" in the rapid waters below.

"Wait a minute. I want to turn him around. He's a dead weight this way and I'm afraid we won't get him over," cautioned Ned.

After much effort he succeeded finally in turning Stacy around so that they could clasp hands.

"Now brace your feet, Chunky, and help all you can."

This Stacy did gladly enough.

"Don't drop me," he warned.

"If somebody doesn't let go you'll be all right," was the comforting answer.

Walter, being weaker than the others, was by this time well-nigh exhausted, but he held on with a determination that did him credit. At last they succeeded in pulling Ned and Chunky to the surface. Both boys were thoroughly exhausted by the time they were hauled up, and for a moment they lay breathing hard.

"Lucky my pants didn't rip, wasn't it?" grinned Chunky. "Did you see me fall in? But where's Tad?" he exclaimed, suddenly sitting up.

The Professor had already hurried to the edge as soon as he was able to get his breath, calling loudly into the depths.

There was no answer. Then the boys added their voices to his, but without result.

Tad could hear them call, but as yet he did not possess the strength to answer. When the rope parted he realized instantly that he was falling, and sought desperately to check his fall. He was powerless to do so. However, the rope did this for him to a certain extent, catching here and there in crevices in the rocks, jolting Tad almost into unconsciousness as he bounded up and down. Finally the springing rope bounced him clear of the last jagged points, dropping him neatly into the bushes.

Tad landed squarely on the pack that he had gone in search of, but the shock was so severe that for a time he lay stunned and motionless.

When finally he became conscious he heard his companions far above calling.

The lad tried and tried to answer them, to assure them that he was safe, but the roar of the stream beside him seemed to drown his weakened voice.

"I've got to make them hear. I simply must make them hear," he said to himself. "They will be beside themselves with worry, believing that I am killed."

Finding that he could not raise his voice sufficiently to carry to the top of the cliff, the lad struggled to his feet and began waving his handkerchief.

At first those above were so busy using their voices that they did not observe the tiny piece of cloth.

They had about given up hope of finding the boy alive, when Ned Rector, who had been anxiously peering into the gorge, suddenly raised himself to his knees.

"I see something moving," he shouted.

The others crowded around him as close to the edge as they dared. They were able to make nothing of what he saw.

"It's Tad! It's Tad!" He's signaling us," cried Ned eagerly.

"Are you sure?" asked the Professor doubtfully.

"Come and see for yourself," answered Ned, grasping the Professor by the arm and rushing him to the edge.

"Be careful! Be careful! You'll have both of us over there, next thing you know."

"Judging from the experiences of our friends, it wouldn't do us much harm," laughed Ned. "There's Tad Butler down there. Goodness knows how far he fell, and Chunky got a bump that would have knocked the breath out of almost anyone. Hooray, T-a-d!" roared Ned in answer to his companion's signal. "Are you all right?"

The tiny piece of cloth waved more emphatically.

"What's the matter, can't you talk?"

The handkerchief fluttered more rapidly.

Ned interpreted this as meaning that the boy could not

make himself heard.

"I am afraid he is hurt."

"Can't be very seriously or he would be unable to stand up and swing that rag," suggested Walter.

"Looks to me as if he were trying to climb up the rocks," announced Chunky.

As they gazed down intently they discovered Tad emerging from the bushes, slowly making his way upward.

"He never can make it," breathed the Professor, anxiously. "He will be killed if he tries it."

"Trust Tad. He knows what he is about. He won't try to climb up here," returned Ned.

"You'll see what he's up to in a minute."

The lad's object in scaling the steep wall as far as he could was to get away from the roar of the water that was hurling itself furiously through the gorge, so he could talk with his companions.

After ascending as far as the formation of the rocks would allow, Tad perched himself behind a point of limestone and swung his hand gayly to those above.

"You can't kill a Pony Rider," glowed Ned.

"Yes, judging from what we have been through, you young gentlemen seem to be immune to almost everything. Of course there is liable to be a first time.

We don't want that to happen. But we have a serious difficulty on hand at the present moment. Call to Master Tad. See if he is all right."

Ned did so.

"I got a pretty fair shaking up," answered Tad, in a voice that they could catch only by the most careful attention.

"How far did you fall?" shouted Walter.

"I didn't have time to measure the distance," answered the voice from below.

The boys uttered a shout of laughter.

"Neither did Chunky."

"What happened to him?"

"He fell over in trying to catch the rope and save you."

"Good boy! Hurt him any?"

"No. It hurt us more in getting him out."

"Ask him if he found the provisions ruined?" suggested the Professor.

Tad informed them that nothing save some of the cooking utensils had been damaged.

All had been too securely packed and wrapped with canvas to insure them against exactly the kind of an accident that had happened.

"Think you can get the stuff up here?" asked Ned.

"I'd like to know how? The rope is all down here. I can't very well throw the things up to the top of the mountain," replied Tad.

"That's so. We had forgotten that," muttered the Professor. "And young gentlemen, will you tell me how Master Tad himself is going to get back? Don't you see my judgment was right when I said it was a dangerous undertaking?"

"It seems so," answered Ned ruefully. "But there must be some way to get the provisions out."

"Bother the provisions," interrupted the Professor, impatiently. "We've something more important than food to consider just now. Master Tad is down in the canyon and from the present outlook he is liable to remain there for some time. Any of you think of a plan that will help us? Here, Eagle-eye, perhaps you can tell us how to get that young gentlemen out of there."

The Indian shrugged his shoulders indifferently.

"Him stay. Spirits git um bymeby."

"You stop that kind of talk," commanded Ned.

"Tad is calling," interrupted Walter.

"What is it?" asked Ned.

"Get a rope and let down here."

"There is not ten feet of rope in the outfit."

"Send for help then. I've got to get out of here somehow."

"Tell him there is no help that we could depend upon, within twenty or thirty miles of here," said the Professor.

CHAPTER VI

MAKING THE BEST OF IT

They were well along in the afternoon now and their predicament was apparently serious.

"There seems to be only one way out of the difficulty," said the Professor, after a little thought.

"What's that, Professor?" asked Walter.

"We must send for help, distant as it is."

"If you will pardon my differing with you, Professor, we have help in plenty right here and a lazy Indian thrown in for good measure," said Chunky.

The boys laughed and nodded their heads in approval.

"What we need is a rope, not more help. Don't you think so?"

"Yes, yes. I should have put it that way myself only -"

"Why not send the Indian for a rope?" suggested Chunky. "I would go myself if I knew the way."

"No, you'd fall in somewhere," chuckled Ned.

"And the Indian probably would forget to come back," added Walter. "Altogether we are in a fix."

"I think Master Stacy's suggestion is the most practicable of all," decided the Professor.

"Yes, but where could you send Eagle-eye?" asked Ned. "It would take two days for him to ride to Springfield, and that much more time to return. Tad would starve to death before that, wouldn't he?"

"Not hardly. Altogether, the situation has some humor in it. Master Tad is down there with plenty of food, but he cannot get up here. On the other hand we are up here safe, but without food and cannot get down to him."

"If Tad couldn't get out, he'd be even better off than we then," laughed Walter.

"We would all be all right in that event, my boy. Come here, Eagle-eye."

The Indian obeyed the command lazily.

"We want you to take one of the ponies and ride back to your friend's place as fast as you can. Get a rope, one long enough to reach down into the gully. Don't spare the pony. Get back as quickly as possible."

"Him no got rope."

"How do you know? You go just the same and you go in a hurry. Don't you dare to show your face back here unless you bring a rope, sir. If you get back before dark, I shall make you a present of this rifle that you have admired so much -"

"I beg your pardon, that's my gun you are trying to give away," objected Stacy.

"Never mind, you shall have another. Don't you think it's worth that much to get Master Tad out of his difficulty quickly?"

"Of course it is. I didn't mean it just that way. Sure, give the lazy Indian my gun, give him anything I have, only do something to make him hurry."

The Indian's eyes sparkled with anticipation. "You give Indian gun?" he asked. "Yes. Me ride um pony like fire from sky."

"Well, get off now," said the Professor. "We'll take for granted that you'll do your best. But get back before dark."

The red man was off with a bound, and releasing one of the ponies leaped into the saddle, plunging over the rough, rocky trail at a pace that threatened destruction to pony and rider.

"They'll break their necks. But he certainly is making time," grinned Walter.

"Hope he doesn't break any necks until he returns with a rope. I don't care how soon after that he -"

"That's not a kind thing to say, even of an Indian," corrected the Professor.

"Then I won't say it. I'll just think it," laughed Ned.

"We have sent for a rope, Tad," called Walter. "You must have patience, for it may be several hours before he gets back."

"Whom did you send?"

"The noble red man," interjected Ned, with a laugh.

"Then, it is more likely to be a week before he returns," sighed the lad.

They could almost hear Tad groan. However, there was nothing they could do, and after talking back and forth for a time, the boys settled down to rest, rather worn out from the excitement of the last few hours.

Chunky, though, seemed drawn to the edge of the cliff as if by some invisible force. He simply could not keep away from it.

Twice Ned Rector had hauled him back.

"Fall over if you wish to, Chunky. I can't be bothered to watch you all the time," said Ned finally.

"I won't fall over. Once is enough," replied Stacy, then they left him to himself.

The boy, observing that his friends were not looking, began to toss tiny pebbles over. He was chuckling with glee. First he would throw one, peer over to watch the effect, then dodge back. Stacy Brown's sense of humor seemed impossible to satisfy.

At first Tad paid little attention, believing that what he heard dropping about him was particles dislodged from the rocks overhead.

But when finally, a bit of limestone the size of a chestnut hit the lad fairly on the top of his head and bounded off, he sprang up from where he had been sitting, with an exclamation of impatience.

Moving slightly to one side, Tad peered cautiously upward. He was gratified a moment later by a sight of Stacy Brown's red face peeking over at him.

"Hi, yi, yi, yi!" exploded Tad Butler.

Just at this time Professor Zepplin happened to cast his eyes over toward Stacy and, seeing that something unusual was going on, went quickly but silently over to the boy.

"What's the trouble? Anything the matter?" called the Professor.

"There will be if you don't tie Chunky to a tree or something," called Tad.

"We haven't any rope to tie him with, but we'll attend to the young man," answered the Professor. "See here, boy, what have you been up to?"

"I - I was tossing pebbles over at him," answered Stacy whimsically.

"That will do, young man," warned the Professor. "I shall have to take you in hand if I hear any more such complaints. Do you know that you might have seriously injured Master Tad? Anything thrown from such a height strikes with considerable force."

Stacy hung his head, and thrusting his hands in his pockets walked away, after which there was peace in the camp of the Pony Riders for some time.

"Every time I try to have a little fun I get into trouble," muttered the boy. "I'll show them some of these days that Stacy Brown isn't the tenderfoot they seem to think he is. I'll do something yet."

He had already done so when he threw himself on the rope with the hope of saving his companion from a terrible fall. But, as usual, his effort had resulted in his own undoing.

"Got anything to eat?" he asked, approaching the group.

"You deserve to go hungry," retorted Ned.

"Looks as though he would, whether he deserves it or not," added Walter.

"Young men, there are some canned beans in my saddle bag. I carried them along in case we should become separated from our pack train," observed the Professor.

"Hooray!" laughed Ned, tossing his hat in the air. "I guess we won't starve this evening. Let's cook them?"

"What shall we cook them in?" asked Walter.

"That's so. I'd forgotten that. Our cooking outfit is at the bottom of the gorge."

"I think you will find something on one of the two

remaining mules - something that will answer the purpose," suggested the Professor. "But first, I would suggest that you unpack your tents and pitch them. It is plain that we shall have to remain here all night."

"Why not throw Tad's tent down to him if we don't succeed in getting him up?" asked Chunky.

"Don't you think we've got enough to do with getting him and the provisions up, without throwing down the rest of our stuff?" sniffed Ned. "You must think we have an easy job ahead of us. Well, if you think that you're wrong; we haven't."

They got to work at once, unloading their tents. The canvas was soon spread out on the ground, ropes laid in place and folding cots placed where they belonged. The next task was to cut some tent poles, which was quickly accomplished. Shortly afterwards, the little tents sprang up, and the boys busied themselves with making them inhabitable.

While they were doing this, Professor Zepplin had busied himself with gathering firewood. He had trouble in finding enough dry stuff to answer their purpose. Walter remembered having seen some in a gully a short distance away.

"I know where it is. I'll go fetch it as soon as we have finished here," he said.

"Very well, Walter. I have enough here to start the supper with."

Having done all that was necessary to the tent for the time being, Walter Perkins ran off to get the wood for the night fire, while Ned, having found a spider, prepared to cook the supper.

Out of the packs he had drawn a small package that looked good to him. He opened it and uttered a shout.

"Will we starve to-night? I guess not," he laughed, waving the contents of the package above his head.

"What have you found?" asked the Professor.

"Bacon. Enough for all of us and perhaps some to spare."

"Then, we are not so badly off after all, Master Ned. How about the coffee?"

"Coffee went down the hill."

"The tea also?"

"Yes. The whole business. Neither have we any butter or lard. We shall have to cook the beans in themselves and eat them without seasoning."

"Cook the bacon with them. That will furnish the salt," suggested Stacy.

"Large head," laughed Ned. "I'll do it. Go fetch me some water."

Stacy hurried away whistling, and in a few minutes returned with his sombrero filled with clear, cool mountain water.

"Here, here! What do you mean? Think we want to

drink out of that old hat?" jeered Ned. "Get a pail; what ails you?"

"Nothing ails me. It's the pail you want to find fault with - not with me."

"What do you mean?"

"The pail's down at the bottom of the mountain with Tad," grinned Stacy.

"That's one on me," laughed Ned. "Very well, go wash the hat thoroughly. I suppose we shall have to use it for a water pail. A good scrubbing won't do it any harm, at that."

"I did wash it," replied Stacy. "Think I'd bring you water in it without doing so?"

"All right, put it down," said Ned, turning away.

"I can't."

"Why not?"

"If I put the hat down the water will all run out over the top."

"Then stand there and hold it till we get through supper," growled Ned, turning to the fire where the bacon was frying in the pan of beans.

Stacy eyed him questioningly for a few seconds, and then with an exclamation poured the water on the ground, jamming the wet, dripping sombrero down over his head.

"You go get your own water. I'm not the cook, anyhow," he said, thrusting both hands into his trousers pockets and strolling over to the other side of the fire, where he watched the supper preparations out of the corners of his eyes.

"Serve you right if we didn't give you any supper," commented Ned.

"I'll set the table if you will agree not to find fault with the way I do it," offered the boy.

"Go ahead. I'll promise."

Stacy flirted the table cloth in the air, and after walking around several times, succeeded in smoothing it out. He could find only two spoons in their kit, and no knives and forks.

The boy pondered deeply for a moment, then hurried off into the brush, returning shortly, stuffing something in his inside coat pocket.

"Grub pi-i-i-lee!" announced the cook.

"Hey, Tad, supper's ready," shouted Ned, peering over the cliff.

"All right," came back the answer. "I'm eating mine now. I've got corned beef and -"

"And what? It must be something pretty good."

"It is. What would you say to canned peaches?"

"Canned peaches! Now, fellows, what do you think of

that? I didn't know there were any in the pack," mourned Ned.

"And you the cook! I don't think you're much of a cook after all. It's lucky for us you didn't know it, I guess," said Stacy, with a grimace.

"Lucky for Tad, you mean. Precious little of those canned peaches we'll ever see. Come, fall to. You'll make me late with my dishes," urged Ned.

They were hungry enough, and the spiderful of beans and bacon looked good to them.

"What, do we have to eat with a spoon - a large spoon, at that?"

"You do, unless you prefer to use your fingers, Professor. We are not allowed by you to do that, but I presume you can if you want to. Chunky doesn't need any. We will divide the two spoons between the three of us," said Ned, with a twinkle in Stacy's direction.

But his levity did not disturb the fat boy in the least. After having had his plate heaped with beans and bacon, Stacy calmly took from his pocket two sharp sticks that he had cut and trimmed just before supper. On one of these he speared a piece of bacon, stringing several beans on the other, and carrying both mouthward at the same time.

The boys burst out laughing.

"Well, will you look at the chopsticks!" exclaimed Ned. "I always thought he'd make a good Chinaman."

"Master Stacy is at least resourceful," answered the Professor, a broad grin on his face. "I think I shall cut me some sticks just like those."

The boy stripped the beans from one into his mouth and extended the stick to Professor Zepplin.

"No, thank you," laughed the scientist. "I think I prefer to get my own."

Chunky solemnly chased a truant bean about his plate, finally spearing and conveying it to his already well-filled mouth.

CHAPTER VII

BOY AND PONIES STRANGELY MISSING

After all, the supper proved a very jolly meal, now that they were sure Tad was all right. Then, again, the beans and bacon were pronounced excellent by each of them, and Stacy had made fully as good time with his crude chopsticks as had the others with the tablespoons.

Supper finished, all hands turned in to help wash the dishes, and in a few moments the camp was again in perfect order.

Tad was informed of Stacy's skill with chopsticks, and they could hear him laughing over it, even though they were no longer able to see him.

"Are you warm enough down there?" called Ned.

"Sure thing. I have most of the blankets."

"That means we freeze, I guess," interjected Stacy.

"You can go cut yourself a few chopsticks and sleep under them," retorted Ned Rector. "Hey, Tad, why don't you build a fire down there?"

"Haven't any matches."

"Never mind, Tad, the moon soon will be up and you can get warm by that," shouted the fat boy.

"Chunky has suddenly developed into a wit, Tad. I don't know what's happened to the boy. It must have been that fall over the cliff that shook his thinking machinery into place."

"Pity some other folks not more'n a million miles away wouldn't fall over," muttered Stacy.

"What's that you say?" demanded Ned, turning on him.

"I - I was just thinking to myself," explained Chunky, edging away.

Ned was glaring at him ferociously, at the same time struggling to keep back the laughter that rose to his lips because of Stacy's sharp retort.

"I'll make a suggestion, young gentlemen," said the Professor.

"Yes, sir, what is it?" asked the boys in chorus.

"Pile up all the dry wood that Walter has gathered. Pile it right up on the edge of the cliff and light it. I think that will make the evening more cheerful for Master Tad down there."

"That will be fine," cried Walter.

Quickly carrying the dried wood to the place indicated, they piled it so that it would make a long fire, then lighted it from three sides at the same time.

The result was a bright blaze that flared high, lighting the rocks far down into the canyon, but not sufficiently far to reach Tad.

"Trying to burn up the mountain?" shouted Tad.

"No; we're trying to burn it down, so we can pick you up," called Ned Rector.

"Oh," came up from the depths.

"It seems to me that you young men are getting rather sharp with each other," said the Professor, shaking his head.

"I guess it must be the Ozark air getting into our lungs," answered Ned. "I've felt like having a wrestling bout with some one ever since we got into these mountains."

"Wait till Tad comes up. I think he will accommodate you," suggested Chunky wisely.

"You mustn't mind our talk, Professor," explained Walter. "We say things to each other, but it's all in fun. We don't mean to be mean. Do we, Ned?"

"Of course not. Chunky is the only one who -"

"Never mind Chunky. He'll take care of himself," answered the fat boy sharply.

"Isn't it about time that lazy Indian were back, Professor?" asked Walter.

"Yes, that's so. I hadn't thought of that, Walter. He has been gone all of five hours now, and the trip should not have taken him more than three all told."

"Suppose he had to stop to smoke a pipe of peace with his friend," suggested Ned. "Then there would be a certain amount of grunting to do before Eagle-eye could state his business, and after that much talk, talk. That's the Indian of it."

"You seem to know a lot about Indians. Were you ever an Indian?" asked Stacy innocently.

"Even if I were, I couldn't be called a savage," retorted Ned.

The hours wore on, and the moon came up in a cloudless sky, much to the relief of the boy down in the canyon. Just before dark he had observed that there was quite a strip of rock and sand on his side of the rushing mountain torrent. It extended further than he could see and the lad wondered where it might lead to.

After a time he cuddled up, but could not sleep. Perhaps it was the loneliness of his position. Yet he had been alone in mountain and forest many times before.

"Hello, up there!" he shouted, pulling himself to a sitting position.

"Hello!" answered Walter.

"I'm going to bed. Don't worry about me. I suppose the Indian has not returned?"

"No such luck," answered Ned, who had come up beside Walter and replied to Tad's question.

"And he won't be back till morning," sang the boy down there in the shadows.

"Right you are," laughed Ned. "If he gets back then we are in great luck. I'll let the rope down to you if he should happen to return during the night."

"No; wait till morning. I wouldn't care to try to climb up in the dark. I'd be likely to get hurt if I did. You had better all turn in now. There will be no need for you to sit up."

"All right," answered Ned and Walter at once.

"I think perhaps Master Tad is right. We had better go to bed. I would suggest, however, that one of you roll up in his blankets outside here, so that he can hear if Master Tad calls," suggested Professor Zepplin.

"That's a good idea. I'll do that, with your permission, Professor," offered Ned Rector promptly.

"Yes. Then Walter and Stacy had better go to their tents. If anything occurs during the night, remember you are to let me know at once. If Eagle-eye returns, I want to know it, too."

"Very well, sir," answered Ned.

After replenishing the fire, determined to remain awake until daylight, the lad rolled up in his blankets.

In a few minutes after the camp quieted down he fell

sound asleep; and he did not open his eyes again until the sun peeped over the eastern range of the mountains and burned apart his eyelids.

Ned awoke with a start. He could scarcely believe that another day had dawned.

He sat up, rubbing his eyes and blinking in the strong morning light.

"Whew! I'm stiff in every joint," he mumbled. "And sleepier than Stacy Brown ever thought of being."

Ned pulled himself to his feet, yawning broadly.

"That's another bad habit I have learned from Chunky. I wonder if Tad's awake."

Peering over the edge, Ned was unable to make out whether his companion down there were awake or sleeping. He hesitated to call, knowing that if Tad Butler were still asleep at that hour of the day it was because he was tired out and needed rest badly.

Ned strode over to Stacy's tent.

"Wake up," he commanded, pinching one of the fat boy's big-toes.

"Get out," mumbled Stacy sleepily, at the same time kicking viciously with the disturbed foot.

Thus encouraged, Ned pulled the other big-toe.

Chunky rose in his wrath, hurling the rubber pillow on which he had been sleeping full into the face of his tormentor.

Ned, caught off his balance, tumbled over in a heap, while Stacy crawled back under the blankets, very well satisfied with the result of his throw.

But he was left in peace only a moment. Ned recovered himself and returned to the charge. Over went the cot, with Stacy beneath it. From the confusion of blankets emerged the red face of the fat boy.

Ned Rector thought it time to leave. He did so, with Stacy a close second and the rubber pillow brushing Ned's cheek in transit.

There was no more sleep in the camp. Ned and Stacy's foot race continued until both were out of breath and thoroughly awake. Then they sat down, laughing, the color flaming in their cheeks and eyes sparkling with pleasurable excitement.

"I'll wake up Tad, I guess," announced Ned after recovering his breath.

Going to edge of the cliff, he shouted loudly. But there was no answer to his summons. Then both boys added their voices to the effort, joined a few minutes later by the Professor and Walter Perkins.

They were unable to get any reply at all; nor was there the slightest movement or sign of life where Tad had last been seen.

"What can it mean?" they asked each other, all the laughter gone out of their faces now.

"It means," said Ned, "that Tad isn't there. Beyond that, I would not venture an opinion."

"Maybe he's fallen into the stream during the night and drowned," suggested Chunky.

"We shall not even consider that as possible, nor do I believe it is," replied the Professor. Nevertheless, he was deeply concerned over the mysterious disappearance of the lad.

"If the Indian ever gets here with a rope, I'll go down there and see if I can find out anything," said Ned.

"Not until all other means have been exhausted," declared the Professor. "We appear to have lost one boy, and I do not intend that we shall lose another."

"I wouldn't worry," comforted Walter Perkins. "You all know Tad, and you know he isn't a boy that you can lose so easily. I'll bet my share in the next meal that he's back here before dark this afternoon."

This confidence brightened the others visibly.

"That's right," agreed Ned. "You can't down Tad. I guess I'll go water my pony and give him some fresh trees to eat up while some of you are starting the fire. We had better eat, anyway."

"What is there to eat?" asked the Professor.

"Beans, that's all, and not much of that. Unless we get the stuff down there, we won't have another meal today."

The other two boys began preparing for the camp-fire. Ned had been gone only a few moments when he returned on a run.

"Boys! Boys!" he cried.

"What is it? What is it?" they exclaimed in sudden alarm.

"The ponies! The ponies!"

"What about them?" asked Walter, pausing as he was about to strike a match to the wood.

"Yes, what of them, Master Ned? Has anything happened to them?" asked the Professor, striding toward the excited Ned Rector.

"Happened? I should say there had -"

"Well, what is it? Don't keep us waiting in suspense all -"

"They're gone!"

"Gone?" exclaimed the two boys in chorus.

"It can't be possible."

"Two of them are. They have broken away, I think. It must have happened late last night, for I looked at them just before going to bed, and they were all asleep then."

"Whi - which ponies - which ones are gone?" asked Walter apprehensively.

"Chunky's and Tad's."

"Is it possible?" sputtered the Professor, striding to the place where their stock had been tethered.

"Yes, they've broken away," he decided, observing that a piece of stake rope belonging to each had been broken short off. "Look around, boys. They cannot be far away. Probably got hungry and concluded to look for some tender bushes to browse on."

The boys, thus encouraged, hastened to begin their search for the missing stock.

"They went this way," shouted Ned.

All hands hurried to him.

"Yes, there's their tracks," agreed the Professor. "Now follow them, but look out that you do not get lost."

Instead, a few moments afterward, they lost the trail. It disappeared from before them as utterly as if the ponies had walked on air from that point on. No amount of searching brought it to view again, and after more than an hour of persistent effort, the Professor called the hunt off, and the crestfallen party returned to camp.

"What are we going to do?" asked Stacy dolefully.

"I know what you are going to do," returned Ned.

"What?"

"You're going to ride a mule from this point on."

CHAPTER VIII

THE INDIAN MAKES A DISCOVERY

It was not a cheerful breakfast to which the lads sat down. It seemed as if nothing but trouble had overtaken them ever since they had been in the Ozark Mountains.

They had just finished when the Indian rode in on Ned's mount, which he had chosen for his journey.

This was something at least to detract their attention from their troubles.

"Hey, you haven't got back, have you?" taunted Ned, noting the flecks of foam on his pony with disapproving eyes.

"Me back," grinned the Indian.

"I see you are," replied the Professor dryly. "Where's the rope?"

"Yes; we don't care so much about seeing you, but we want that rope," added Ned emphatically.

"No got um."

"Do you mean to say you have been gone nearly twenty-four hours and have not found a rope?" demanded Professor Zepplin.

"No rope," persisted the guide sullenly.

"Why not?" demanded Ned, steadying himself, for he was more wrought up than he wished to admit, even to himself.

The Shawnee shrugged his shoulders.

"Where's that rope?" snapped Chunky, with sudden new-found courage, facing the guide at close quarters.

"No get um! No get um!" insisted the Indian, gesticulating extravagantly.

"Yes, but why not, why not?" urged the Professor.

"No find."

"You mean you could not find one?"

"He doesn't know what he means," sneered Ned. "He's had too much pipe of peace."

"Go take care of that pony," commanded the Professor sternly. "Rub him down well. After you have done so, return and get your breakfast. There's not much for you."

"He'll have to wash his own dishes," announced Ned. "No washing dishes for a lazy Indian. No, not for me."

"Yes, he will have to do that," agreed the Professor.

"Come back here, Eagle-eye."

The boys did not know at the moment what the Professor had in mind.

"Two of our ponies got away last night, Eagle-eye."

The Indian nodded, but without exhibiting any surprise.

"Did you know it?"

"Me know."

"How?" demanded the Professor, with unfeigned surprise.

"Me see um tracks. Me see um ropes there."

"Well, you have got some sense after all,'" retorted the Professor. "How do you suppose they got away?"

"No get away."

"What's that? What do you mean?" asked Ned sharply.

"No get away."

"I guess the pipe of peace has gone to his head," declared Ned disgustedly. "Now you say they didn't get away. If not, they must be over there now. How do you explain that?"

"No there."

"Of course they're not. Then they got away."

"No get away. Steal um," announced the Indian calmly.

His announcement was like an electric shock to them.

"Stolen? Stolen? Is that what you mean?" shouted Professor Zepplin.

"Yes."

"Oh, preposterous! Stolen? And with all of us sleeping within a rod or so of them? Impossible."

"Eagle-eye say stole," insisted the guide.

"How do you know?"

"See um tracks, then not see um tracks."

"Well, what do you infer from that - what does that mean?"

The Indian went through a series of pantomimic gestures to indicate that the feet of the missing ponies had been bound with cloths so that their hoofs would leave no imprint.

"Come Eagle-eye," he commanded, striding off toward the bedding-down place.

They followed and gathered around him as he picked up the ends of the tether ropes.

"Break um? No, cut um."

"You mean the ropes have been cut?"

"Uh-huh," he grunted in gutteral tones.

There was silence for a moment.

"He isn't such a wooden Indian as he'd have us believe after all," grinned Ned.

"Can't you trail them?" asked Stacy.

The Shawnee shook his head.

"Why not?"

"No leave trail. Smart man."

"Yes, there is no doubt of that," agreed the Professor. "Have you any idea who did this thing, Eagle-eye?"

The Shawnee shrugged his shoulders as indicating that he did not know.

"Probably it was the same fellow whom you found fooling about the camp the other night," suggested Walter.

"Just what I was thinking," added Ned.

"Yes, no doubt he is the man. But what we are going to do, I don't know. It occurs to me that I might send some one on to Mr. Munson, superintendent of the Red Star Mine, to whom I have a letter, asking him to send us on a couple of extra ponies."

"Does he know who we are?" asked Walter Perkins.

"Yes, he knows your father. Mr. Munson is expecting

us, and is to entertain us when we reach the place."

"How far are we from there now?" inquired Ned.

"How far, Eagle-eye?"

"Two suns."

"Two days, eh. We could make it while Eagle-eye was going there and back. I move that we wait until to-morrow. Perhaps we may find Tad some time to-day. I believe he will return, as I said before. If he does, we can start right on. Some of us will have to walk, but that doesn't matter. We are pretty well used to doing that, I guess."

"Master Ned, your suggestion is a good one. We shall adopt it. I presume the other animals are safe. The thieves certainly will not have the assurance to come back again."

"No come more," affirmed the guide.

"After you have finished your breakfast I want you to start in and look for Master Butler. You'll have to find a way to get down there, even if you have to wade in the stream -"

"Spirits git um boy."

"We will leave that out of the question. You find him, that's all."

"He won't go down there," said Ned. "He may say he will, but he won't."

"I'll see that he does," replied the Professor, with a firm closing of the lips. "I have trifled long enough. Now we shall do something. I -"

"Well, what's all the excitement about?" demanded a cheery voice behind them.

"Tad! It's Tad!" shouted the boys in chorus.

With yells of delight they pounced upon him and for a moment there was a regular football scrimmage, with Tad Butler at the bottom of the heap, the others mauling him about with shouts of glee.

It was the Pony Rider Boys' way of showing their delight at the return of their companion. But Tad did not mind it at all. Throwing them off with a prodigious effort he scrambled to his feet, dust-covered, hatless and with hair in a sad state of disorder.

Professor Zepplin had thrust the other boys aside and was gripping Tad's hands.

"It's the last time you ever get me to consent to your taking such a chance," he said. "How did you get out? You certainly did not climb up the side of the mountain."

"Oh, no," laughed Tad. "I knew there must be some way out, for I found a moccasin track down there in the sand before I turned in last night."

"You must have pretty good eyes to find a moccasin track in the dark," laughed Ned.

"I did not say it was dark. I made the discovery

before that."

"Tell us about it," urged Walter.

"You didn't find any of Eagle-eye's evil spirits down there, did you?" asked Ned.

"No. I wish I had. I should have been glad of company of any kind."

"We want to hear how you got out," spoke up Chunky. "I - I came pretty near falling in after you, too."

"Yes, I know. Well, to begin with, before I found the moccasin track I noticed that there was room to walk along by the side of the stream. When the moon came up, not being able to sleep, for some reason - I guess it was on account of the water that made such a racket, I thought I'd look around a bit. After I got started I kept on going and going, and the further I went the less steep did the banks appeared -"

"How far did you go?" interrupted the Professor.

"I haven't the slightest idea."

"I presume you found no great change in the topographic features of -"

Tad laughed good-naturedly.

"I was trying to get out, Professor. Finally, I found a place that looked good and after I had scrambled up some fifteen feet I discovered that I had struck a trail. It had been in use not long since. What for I cannot imagine. The rest was very easy. I reached the top of the cliff just after daylight."

"How - how did you find your way back?" wondered Stacy.

"I followed along the ridge. After a while I saw the smoke from your camp-fire, then I hurried in and here I am."

"You always were a lucky fellow," laughed Ned. "Now if that had been myself I should have been down there yet, or else in the river or whatever you call that stream down there."

"Got anything to eat?" asked Tad. "My appetite this morning is a thing to be feared."

"Depends upon how much the guide has eaten," replied Walter. "I guess you will have to lick the frying pan."

"Yes, that's all he'll get," added Ned. "Any fellow who has filled up on canned peaches and the like doesn't need any more than that."

"Professor," continued Tad, "I would suggest that we pack up and move along down until we come to the trail. We can all then work into the gorge leaving the ponies on top. It will be an easy matter for us to pack the stuff to the top. We'll be in good shape then. Shall we do it?"

"Yes, yes," answered the Professor absently.

"Come on then, fellows. I'll tighten my belt and save my appetite until we get something like real food to eat. Licking a frying pan won't satisfy my longings this morning. I'll pack the ponies while you are striking the tents. I -"

Tad turned, gazing at them curiously. They were strangely silent. The lad felt instinctively that something had gone wrong, for Tad Butler was quick to catch a suggestion.

"Well, what is it all about? You are as solemn as a lot of owls at sunrise. Anything happened?"

Walter nodded.

"It's about the ponies, Master Tad," the Professor informed him.

"The ponies? Which ponies? Are they hurt?" exclaimed the lad sharply.

"We don't know," answered Professor Zepplin.

"Then what is the matter? Don't keep me in suspense."

"Gone," growled Ned dismally.

"Where?"

"I'm sure I don't know. The redskin says they have been stolen - your pony and Chunky's. The trail has been masked so we cannot follow them."

Without a word, Tad Butler hastened to the spot where the animals had been tethered when he went over the cliff. Silently he made a careful inspection of the place.

"Well, what do you think of it?" asked Ned.

"I think I'll walk," answered Tad, thrusting both hands in his trousers pockets. "But I'm going to get my pony back before ever I leave these mountains," he announced quietly.

CHAPTER IX

HORSE THIEVES PAY A SECOND VISIT

Tad was unusually silent while they were packing ready to break camp, but as they got out on the trail he became more talkative. He did not refer to the ponies again on the way, though the lad's mind was working rapidly.

"Do you think we shall be able to hire some ponies of Mr. Munson?" he asked when they had been an hour on their journey.

"I have no doubt of it," answered the Professor. "Perhaps it would be better to buy a couple."

"I don't want to do that just yet. There's the place where we are to leave the trail," he added, pointing to what appeared to be a broad gash in the rocks ahead of them. "We shall have to leave the ponies, what few we have left. I don't suppose the thieves will come back for the rest of them, do you?"

"Hardly," answered the Professor.

Securing their mounts as well as the two pack mules, they started down the mountain side with Tad Butler in the lead. On down the long, sloping trail they trudged until at last they reached the point where they were obliged to get down on all fours to clamber the last fifteen feet of precipitous rocks.

Eagle-eye halted, standing rigid, gazing off across the gorge.

"Well, what are you waiting for?" demanded the Professor. "Come along. We shall need you."

"Me stay."

Professor Zepplin was angry. He was for trying to force the Indian to accompany them.

"I would suggest that you let him remain where he is," said Tad. "We shall need some one here to haul up the packs when we get them at the bottom there. I'll leave my rope for him."

"Very well, just as you say. I hate to see even an Indian make such an exhibition of himself," answered the Professor witheringly. "I never supposed there were such cowards among the red men."

Tad handed his rope to Eagle-eye, at the same time telling the fellow what he was to do. The party then scrambled down the rocks, soon finding themselves on more secure footing by the side of the roaring stream.

The mountain torrent was more of a reality to the boys now than had been the case when they were gazing down upon it from the top of the cliff.

"My, I'd hate to fall in there!" decided Stacy, edging away from the flying spray that floated like a thin cloud along the edge of the bank, masking the torrent like a white veil.

"Wonderful! wonderful!" exclaimed the Professor, raising both hands above his head, glancing first up then down the imposing mountain gash. He was deeply impressed by the spectacle.

"Young gentlemen," he said, turning to them, impressively, "it would be well for you to give serious thought to the remarkable region in which you now find yourselves."

"Yes, sir," agreed Tad.

"We are not liable to forget it, Professor," added Ned.

"The Ozark region is unusual in having within such limited areas so wide a range of geological formation."

Professor Zepplin in his enthusiasm was waxing eloquent, and the lads were giving respectful attention.

"Perhaps you are unaware," continued the scientist, "that in both the eastern and western portions of this range, a section running transversely to its main axis presents a complete succession from the oldest Archaean to the newest quaternary."

The Professor fixed Stacy with a stern eye.

"Do you follow me, young gentleman?"

"Ye - yes, sir," stammered Chunky weakly, shrinking back against the rocks.

"And from perfectly massive rocks to the most perfectly stratified sediments there are represented a considerable variety of masses belonging to different ages - a very complete section of the Palaeozoic and a rather full sequence of the latter deposits which recline against the older strata."

"Yes, sir," agreed Ned meekly.

"A-h-e-m. And now having thus enlightened you, we will proceed with our quest for something to eat. I trust my explanation has been perfectly clear to you all?" queried the scientist, with the suspicion of a twinkle in his eyes.

"With all due respect to you, sir, I must confess that I didn't understand a word of it," answered Tad boldly.

"I hadn't the slightest idea that you did," retorted the Professor, with a hearty laugh. "Our friend, Master Stacy, appears to be the only one of you who grasped the scientific truths."

The boys shouted with laughter.

Ned Rector proposed three cheers for Professor Zepplin, which were given with a will.

Stacy, rather crestfallen, joined in the cheering, weakly, however.

"It is well to give thought now and then to more serious matters, boys. After we are out of our present difficulty I will put what I have just told you into more simple language - language that you will all understand. This is the most unusual country we have been in yet, and I want you to leave it with a pretty clear idea of the lessons it teaches. How far is it to where our provisions were dumped?"

"It will take us an hour to get there, I should say," replied Tad. "We had better be on our way."

Tad tied his red handkerchief to a bush, so they might not miss the trail upon their return, after which the party started out on its long tramp.

"If we were nearer to food, I should not take the time to rescue the supplies. At the present rate, it may be days before we reach a settlement."

"Especially if we lose any more live stock," said Tad.

Lost in admiration, the lads worked their way along the bank, gazing first at the swirling waters, whose spray here and there gave off the colors of the rainbow in the morning sun, then up at the towering white limestone cliffs above them.

"There's the place," announced Tad finally.

"Where?" queried the Professor.

"Just below where you see that projection of rock that looks like an Indian's nose. That's the rock that I tumbled down after the rope broke with me. I am black and blue yet. Don't think there's a spot on the rock that I didn't hit on my way down. My, I got a bump!"

"Are the things damaged?" asked Ned solicitously.

"No, nothing to speak of. I guess I did the most

damage when I helped myself last night," laughed Tad.

Tad, after finishing his meal, had carefully packed the stuff together, and they now found it all in excellent condition. The heavy canvas had protected the food and dishes in the dizzy fall, though some of the cans had been considerably flattened.

"What do you say to having a real breakfast down here?" suggested Walter.

"Yes, I'm hungry," urged Chunky.

"Oh, you'll get over that," retorted Ned.

"An excellent idea, but what are you going to do for a fire?" asked Professor Zepplin.

They had not thought of that before.

"That's so. There is no wood down here at all," said Tad. "But, wait a minute. I know where there are some dead brush stick a little way from here. Come on, some of you fellows, and we'll see what we can do."

When they returned each had his arms full of brush and vines, all of which they dumped in a heap on the edge of the rapids.

"It doesn't look very promising," said the Professor, with a doubtful shake of his head.

"No, I guess it will be a quick fire," answered Tad. "Ned, you get the coffee ready and the other things so we can put them on the fire the moment we get it started. I'll have the pile ready by the time you are."

With considerable skill the lad arranged the heap, placing the dead leaves and the driest of the sticks at the bottom. On top he placed a mass of half green stuff, packing the whole down by throwing himself on the pile, after which he rounded it up in a mound shape, with a circle of stones in the middle.

The fire blazed up encouragingly, and Ned, getting water from the rapids for the coffee, put the pot quickly into the ring of stones.

"Something's going to happen in about a minute," announced Chunky, with an air of great wisdom. He had been watching the preparations with hands thrust deeply into his pockets.

"What's going to happen?" demanded Ned, turning on him sharply.

Chunky, instead of replying, leaned back against the rocks and began to whistle. In a moment the disaster that he had foreseen was upon them.

The flimsy pile of brush and vines, after the fire had burned away its foundations, gave way beneath the weight of the stones. Coffee pot, coffee and stones went down with a crash and a clatter.

"Save the coffee pot!" shouted Ned, giving Chunky a push.

"Save it yourself. I'm not the cook," answered the fat boy, who chanced to be nearest to the fire. "I told you something was going to happen."

In the meantime Tad Butler had sprung to the rescue.

With one well-directed kick he had scattered the brush and rescued the coffee pot before serious damage had been done to it.

Rushing to the river, he scooped up a fresh supply of water, planting the pot in the center of the fire and heaping the burning stuff about it.

"We'll have some coffee after all," he glowed. "I don't think Ned is much of a cook, do you, Chunky?"

"'Bout as good as you are at making fires to cook by, I guess," mumbled Chunky.

Tad laughed with them at his own expense.

The water was soon boiling, however, and with the canned stuff laid on the canvas which had been spread out close to the water, the jolly party shortly after that were able to sit down to breakfast.

"Two lumps of sugar I believe you take, Professor?" questioned Ned politely, poising a handful of lumps over the Professor's cup.

"Give me four," interjected Chunky.

"You take yours clear this morning," retorted Ned.

"I got the condensed milk, anyway," jeered Chunky. "No sugar for me, no condensed milk for you," and he planted the can firmly between his feet, which were curled up half under him.

"Oh, give him the sugar. I have to take my coffee half milk," begged Walter.

"All right, hand over the condensed milk then. I'll give you two lumps," said Ned.

"Three," replied Chunky, firmly, making no move to hand over the milk.

Ned let the lumps drop into his companion's cup, but from such a height that Chunky had to dodge as the coffee flew up.

He wiped a few drops of the coffee from his face, deliberately filled his cup to overflowing with milk, then handed the can to Walter.

"I guess Chunky doesn't need any of our help. He is pretty well able to take care of himself," laughed Tad.

"Delicious," breathed the Professor, sampling his cup of steaming liquid.

"Who, Chunky?" asked Ned quizzically.

"Certainly not the coffee," replied the Professor in a tone of reproof.

The meal was finished with many a jest and the pack divided up into bundles so that each should have his share to carry, after which the lads took up their return tramp.

They arrived at the mountain trail shortly before noon.

"Where's the guide?" asked Tad, glancing about.

"Probably asleep somewhere," replied Ned. "He's almost as big a sleepy head as Chunky."

"He is not here, Ned."

"Most unreliable guide we've had. I shall dismiss him immediately upon our arrival at the Red Star Mine," decided the Professor. "You are sure he is nowhere about, Tad?"

"You can see. He's not here. I hope he has left the rope. I'll climb up there and find out. No, he has taken it with him, evidently."

"Here's the rope," called Stacy, hauling it from a clump of bushes where it had evidently been dropped.

"Coil it and cast it up here," directed Tad.

This done, he began hauling up the bundles that they made fast to it below. Finally, this was completed without accident. All hands took up their packages from that point and started along the winding trail that led up the mountain side.

"Most peculiar, most peculiar," muttered the Professor.

"Maybe some of those spirits that the Indian was talking about came up and got him," suggested Stacy, with serious face.

"Maybe," agreed Ned. "But I'd sooner think they would take you if they were the real bad spirits."

"It is my opinion," declared Professor Zepplin gravely, "that the spirits that trouble Eagle-eye most are not the supernatural kind. We certainly drew a prize when we picked him."

"We did," agreed Tad, laughing.

"Next time we'll choose a white man, if we can get one -"

"Hello, he isn't here, either," called Ned, who was the first to reach the end of the trail at the top.

Tad, close behind him, cast a searching glance about.

"That's not all that is missing, either," he said sharply.

"What!" exclaimed the Professor.

"Two more ponies, that's all," replied Tad Butler. "We are a smart lot to let him steal our stock right under our very eyes."

CHAPTER X

THE PROFESSOR DISTINGUISHES HIMSELF

The boys uttered a cry of dismay.

"You don't mean - you can't mean they have been here again?"

"It looks that way," replied Tad. "Both Walter's and Ned's ponies are gone. See, the ropes have been untied, not cut. The ponies surely did not do that."

The Professor was much too excited to speak for the moment.

"I am glad they did not take your mount, Professor. That is one thing to be thankful for, anyway," said Tad. "I don't understand this business at all."

"Why, they must have been hanging about our camp all the time. They followed us here," exploded Ned. "We are a lot of tenderfeet."

"Some of us," suggested Chunky.

"This is no joke," snapped Ned, turning on him almost savagely. "We are in a fix."

"Yes, but we've got two mules left, haven't we," queried the boy whimsically.

"It's an outrage!" shouted the Professor. "I'll have the law on them whoever they are. They shall suffer for this!"

"Yes, but first we shall have to catch them, Professor," returned Tad. "It seems we were not misinformed when they warned us to be on the lookout for horse thieves."

"In Springfield, yes. I had no idea it was as bad as this. They certainly can't get away without being caught."

"I don't know about that. But I do know that we have been easy game for the thieves."

"Do you think they took anything else?" demanded the Professor.

"I don't see that anything else is missing, do you, Ned?"

"No."

"See, they took off the saddles. Didn't want them for some reason. I'm glad of that. By the way, did they get my saddle when they stole my pony last night?" asked Tad.

"No, I had your saddle in my tent," Walter informed him.

"The question is -" began Tad.

"The first question is, what has become of Eagle-eye," interrupted the Professor.

"That's so. I had forgotten about him," said Tad.

The lads looked at each other questioningly. The same thought was in the mind of each.

"You - you don't suppose -" muttered Walter.

"Of course! That's it! It's Eagle-eye!" exclaimed Ned.

"Don't be too quick to accuse anyone, young gentlemen. It is very irritating, I know. But let us be slow about placing the charge at any man's door, be he copper colored or white."

"But, Professor," expostulated Ned Rector, "he goes away, and while absent from camp two ponies are stolen. To-day we leave him halfway down the rocks and upon our return, two more ponies are missing, as well as the Indian himself. What can we think, but that he has had something to do with our loss?"

"If I remember correctly, it was Eagle-eye who called our attention to the fact that the animals had been stolen last night. You thought they had broken away," recalled Professor Zepplin.

"That's so," agreed Ned.

"It certainly does look bad. If Eagle-eye had no hand in the theft, why should he run away as he seems to have done?" asked Tad.

"This is what is known as circumstantial evidence," the

Professor informed them. "I do not say that the Indian is guiltless. I am simply counseling caution. Wait. We shall soon be at the mines, and from there, we can set the officers of the law on the track, which we shall do as soon as we are able to communicate with Mr. Munson."

"Yes, but how are we going to get there?" asked Ned.

"Guess we'll have to ride the mules," grinned Stacy.

"You may be a mule driver if you wish - I'll walk," retorted Ned.

"That's what we all shall have to do," laughed Tad. "Glad the thieves didn't take our guns."

"And the food," reminded Stacy.

"Yes. Probably they knew you had your appetite with you," laughed Ned.

In the meantime Tad had begun a search about the place for clues. He discovered where the animals had been taken from camp, but, as in the case with the loss of the other animals, the trail suddenly disappeared a short distance from camp.

"They seem to have headed for the west. We are sure of that much," decided Ned.

"Which means nothing at all," answered Tad. "They may have turned and gone back or else are traveling along ahead of us. In either case we can't follow them. Do you not think we had better be starting, Professor? We cannot afford to lose a minute now. I want my pony."

"And so do I - and I - and I," added the lads, one after the other.

"I think so. Yet how are we going to find our way? We shall be lost."

"No, we can't get lost, Professor," interrupted Stacy.

"Not lost - cannot get lost?"

"No."

"Why not?" glared the Professor.

"We can't get lost," announced Stacy impressively, "because we don't know where we are, anyway."

A roar of laughter greeted this assertion. It did more than anything else to put the boys in a better frame of mind - unless perhaps it might have been the return of the lost ponies.

"I am forced to admit the correctness of Master Stacy's logic," replied the scientist, after their laughter had subsided.

"It seems fairly simple to me," spoke up Tad. "The mountains run in a southeasterly direction. If we follow that direction we are bound to come out somewhere -"

"In Arkansas or the Indian Territory or some other place," cut in Ned Rector.

"As I understand it," went on Tad, not heeding the interruption, "these gorges or canyons in the Ozark range follow the same general direction. We have one right here by us, and we have the sun above us. Between the two we should be able to find our way."

"That sounds promising, Master Tad. You are a level-headed young man, even if you do take long chances and do foolish things now and again. I shall adopt your suggestion and we'll be off at once."

They were forced to pack some of their belongings on the back of Professor Zepplin's mount, while each of the two mules was subjected to an additional load.

When the packing had been finished there was little room for anyone to ride, so Tad took one of the mules, Ned Rector the other, leading them by short ropes, and started off followed by Walter and Stacy on foot, with the Professor riding his own pony.

The boys moved away with broad grins on their faces as they thought of the spectacle they were creating. Yet there was none to watch their undignified progress. However, leading a mule and riding a pony were two distinctly different operations. The boys were in a hurry and the mules were not and over this difference of inclination they had many disagreements.

Once Ned lost his temper with the beast of burden that he had in tow, and used his crop rather too freely to suit the long-eared animal. The latter kicked until he kicked the pack from his back.

Amid the shouts of laughter of his companions, his face red and perspiring, Ned was obliged to gather up the pack in sections and strap it in place again, which he did after much endeavor. Thereafter he kept his temper.

"I've heard it said that a mule wouldn't kick after twelve o'clock," said Chunky. "Guess it wasn't true."

"Perhaps it is after twelve o'clock at night that was meant," suggested Tad.

"Mules are asleep then, aren't they?"

"Supposed to be, I guess."

"Then that's it," answered the fat boy somewhat enigmatically.

They failed to make any great distance that day. How far they had advanced they did not know. Shortly before sundown they called a halt at Professor Zepplin's suggestion.

The mules went to sleep while the boys were unloading them. Ned confessed that he was nearly fagged. Tad, on the other hand, declared that he had never felt better in his life.

"Hope they won't steal anymore live stock," said Ned. "If they do we'll have to pack the outfit on our own backs, which, after all, probably wouldn't be any harder than trying to lead a stubborn mule. I think I'll tie a string around the necks of the stock and hitch the string to my big-toe to-night. Then I'll know if anybody tries to run off with them."

"Run off with your big-toes?" queried Chunky.

"No, run off with the ponies, I said - I mean the pony and the mules."

Stacy's eyes lighted up appreciatively.

"I've got a string that you can use," he said. "I'll fix it up for you. Shall I?"

"You would like to see me lose my big-toes, wouldn't you? No, thank you, I'll furnish my own string if I decide to adopt the plan."

After supper had been cooked and eaten, and the dishes washed, all hands gathered around the camp-fire, where they remained until bedtime, which on that particular night was earlier than usual, because all were more or less tired after their active day.

It was decided that some one should be left on guard lest they lose their remaining stock. The Professor took the first half of the night, Tad going on at half past twelve and remaining through the rest of the night.

Nothing occurred to disturb the camp, for which all hands were thankful. Tents were quickly struck after breakfast and once more the outfit started out on the trail after having discussed the advisability of bearing to the west a little. Their final conclusion, however, was to keep within sight of the gorge.

Two days passed as the little outfit crawled along over the rough mountain passes, down through broad deep washes and narrow draws. It was trying work, but the lads kept up their spirits. So inured were they to hardships, by this time, that the unusual strain gave them little or no inconvenience.

On the morning of the third day they had about decided to change the course and try to find their way out of the mountains as the quickest method of getting out of their predicament.

They were gathering their equipment together preparatory to making a start in the new direction, when Tad startled the camp by a sudden exclamation of surprise.

"What is it this time?" cried the Professor, prepared for almost any surprise.

"I see smoke!"

"Oh, is that all," answered Ned disgustedly, not at first realizing the importance of the announcement to them. "I thought maybe you had discovered the missing ponies."

"Perhaps I have. Who knows? At any rate, don't you see it means we are going to meet some human beings at last? We haven't seen one, outside of our own party, in several days, though we have good reason for thinking that one or more has been near us."

"Smoke, smoke?" queried the Professor. "Where?"

"There, to the southwest."

"That's so, it is smoke. It surely is."

"Must be somebody's camp-fire," decided Tad, studying the wisps of vapor that were curling lazily up on the clear, warm morning air.

"Indeed, it must be," declared the Professor. "We must

get in touch with them at once, for they no doubt will soon be on their way. We have not a minute to lose."

The Professor began bustling about excitedly.

"It will be an hour or more before we can hope to get there with our old local freight train," objected Ned. "They probably will be gone long before that."

"Yes. I have it," cried the Professor. "I will hurry over there on my pony. You boys come along at your leisure. Even if they do not wish to wait for the rest of our party, I shall be able to get directions at least, and perhaps to hire some one to pilot us on to the Red Star."

This seemed to be good judgment, so the boys hastened to saddle the Professor's mount, and in a few moments he was jogging away as rapidly as the uneven ground would permit, his eyes fixed on the distant spiral of smoke curling lazily upward.

"Guess we had better follow as fast as we can," suggested Tad.

"Chunky, get busy. What are you standing around with your hands in your pockets for while Rome is burning?" shouted Ned Rector. "Hurry up! Take down those tents, pack all the stuff over to the mules and -"

"And what are you going to do while I'm doing that?" drawled Stacy.

"Me? I'm going to boss the job. What did you suppose I was going to do?"

"Oh, that's about what I thought you would be doing. I'll pack my own stuff. You can leave yours here for all I care," laughed the fat boy, sauntering to his tent without the least attempt to hurry.

"Don't tease him so," advised Tad in a low voice.

"What, tease Chunky Brown? You couldn't tease Chunky with a club. I just say those things to get him started. He says such funny things."

Nevertheless, the camp was struck in record time that morning, and the pack mules loaded so rapidly that they turned back their soulful eyes in mild protest.

"Got a new job for you to-day, Chunky," announced Ned Rector while cinching the pack girths.

"What is it?"

"We've decided to let you follow along behind with a sharp stick and prod the mules so they will make better time."

"Think I'll wait till after twelve o'clock to-night," answered the fat boy.

They were off soon after that, but the mules had never seemed to move as slowly as they did that morning. Instead of an hour, more than two hours had passed before they finally came within hailing distance of the camp-fire. For some time, they had been finding difficulty in keeping it in sight, as the fire appeared to be dying down.

Tad shouted to attract the attention of the campers or

the Professor to let them know the Pony Riders were coming. There was no reply, which caused the lads to wonder.

So they pushed the mules all they could, a vague apprehension that all was not as it should be, growing in their minds. They soon came upon the object of their search. What they found was a smouldering camp-fire.

"The camp is deserted," groaned Tad.

Not a person save themselves was within sight or sound. Professor Zepplin, too, had disappeared.

CHAPTER XI

CHUNKY OBJECTS TO EGG WATER

"Well, doesn't that beat all!" marveled Tad.

"Certainly does," agreed Ned.

"Yes, but I don't understand - what does this mean?" exclaimed Walter.

"I'm a poor guesser," answered Ned.

"It means that we are all alone," replied Tad. "Beyond that I could not guess."

Chunky had been viewing the scene with solemn complacency.

"We've got the mules, anyway," he nodded.

"Precious lot of good they'll do us," returned Walter.

"And we've got the food and - and I don't have to build a fire, either," added the fat boy.

"Yes, we have some things to be thankful for, that's a fact," laughed Tad. "My idea is that the Professor, finding the men had just left here, has hurried on to overtake them. I don't think we have any reason to worry."

"Then we had better stay right here," answered Ned.

"Yes. That is all we can do for the present."

"Think we had better unpack?"

Tad considered the matter briefly.

"I think we had better wait a little while," he decided.

"I think you are right. I hope we don't have to. We have enough food in our pockets to keep us going until night and -"

"Don't we get anything to eat until night?" wailed Chunky.

"Not unless you can browse," retorted Ned. "There's plenty of green stuff hereabouts."

"You can eat with the mules if you wish to. I don't."

"Might as well keep the fire up," decided Tad, gathering up a fresh supply of green stuff which he dumped on the graying ashes. "The smoke will help the Professor to find us quickly when he comes back."

"What if he shouldn't come back?" asked Walter, with sudden apprehension.

"Oh, he will. Don't worry about that. You can't lose the Professor."

The boys laughed, then settled down to make the best of their situation, whiling away the time with jest and stories.

After a time, Tad left the party and strolled from the camp in an effort to determine which way the late occupants of the camp had gone. He was beginning to feel worried, but as yet had confided nothing of this to his companions.

Examining the ground closely he found four distinct trails leading from the abandoned camp. These trails were fresh, showing that ponies had only recently been ridden over them. They all looked alike, however, and he was unable to determine which of them had been made by Professor Zepplin's pony.

"Evidently the party, whoever they were, split up after leaving here," thought the lad aloud. "I'd like to follow out the trails, but I don't dare do so. The Professor would be liable to return while I was away. Then again I might lose the trail and my own way at the same time. I've caused this outfit enough trouble as it is."

With this, Tad slowly turned back toward the camp.

He found a growing sense of uneasiness among his companions there.

"What did you discover?" asked Ned rather more solemnly than was his usual wont.

Tad told him.

"Then, there's no use trying to follow?"

"No."

"What time is it?"

"Half-past three," announced Tad after consulting his watch.

"Huh!" grunted Ned. "I guess the Professor has gone and done it himself this time."

"We'll wait," answered Tad easily.

After piling fresh fuel on the fire Tad went over and sat on the bluff overlooking the eastern slope of the range of mountains which they were traversing. Chunky lay stretched out sound asleep, untroubled by the series of disasters that had overtaken them.

Tad after running over in his mind many plans, none of which seemed practicable, also lay down for a nap, and in a few moments the tired boys were all sound asleep, including the pack mules.

When they awakened the sun had been down all of half an hour. Tad was the first to awake. He started up guiltily, and looking around found that he was not the only one who had napped.

"Hallo, the camp!" he shouted.

The other boys sat up suddenly, rubbing their eyes.

"Time to go to bed. Get up!" laughed Tad.

"Nice way to put it," growled Ned. "Tell a fellow to get up because it's time to go to bed."

"Wat'cher wake me up for?" demanded Chunky. "I was sleeping."

"So were all of us. First time I ever heard you object to being called to eat."

"Eat? Eat? Who said eat?" cried the fat boy, struggling to his feet with difficulty, his head whirling from the effort of pulling himself awake so suddenly.

"I did. It's night."

"You don't say," wondered Ned, looking around in surprise. "I - I thought I was back home in Chillicothe."

"Dreams, dreams," muttered Stacy. "No Professor yet, eh?"

"No. I believe he is lost. He surely would have been back long before this."

"Maybe he's gone the same place the Indian went," ventured Walter.

"Where's that?" queried Stacy, at once interested.

"That's a conundrum. You dream over it to-night," jeered Ned.

"We had better unpack and make camp," advised Tad. "Chunky, Walt and I will do that if you will get the supper."

"All right. Somebody get me some water."

"I will," said Walter quickly. "Anybody know where I can find it?"

"There must be some near by. Those other fellows would not have made camp here and remained all night unless there was water near -"

"Unless they know no more about these confounded mountains than we do, you mean?" laughed Ned.

After some searching about, Walter found a spring. It was full of water that had a whitish tinge to it. The lad tasted it gingerly, then smiled knowingly. Filling his pail he returned to camp with it.

By this time Tad and Stacy had unloaded the mules. The three boys got to work at once putting up the tents. In the absence of Professor Zepplin, they concluded to erect only two, and by the time this had been accomplished, Ned was ready for them.

"Come and get it!" he bellowed.

There was no table cloth, no table, just the bare ground, and the boys sat down to eat in the fresh, bracing air.

"No one who has not been camping for a long time can appreciate smoke," announced Ned oracularly. "If I had to go without my supper I believe if I could breathe smoke for a few minutes, I could almost imagine I had a full stomach."

"Well, I couldn't. I've heard of smoke-eaters, whatever or whoever they are, but I want something a little more lasting," announced Walter Perkins. "No smoked smoke diet for me."

"Nor for me," agreed Tad.

"What's a smoke eater?" asked Stacy.

"I should say that a Pony Rider Boy named Ned Rector was one, according to his own admission," laughed Walter.

"Pass the water, please."

Walter filled Stacy's cup. The fat boy drank it down without taking a breath. No sooner had he swallowed the liquid than he hurled the cup from him and leaped to his feet coughing and making wry faces.

They could not imagine what had happened.

"Slap him on the back, he's choking," shouted Ned.

Walter Perkins, by this time, was laughing immoderately, while his companions were jolting Stacy between the shoulders and shaking him violently.

"Stop pounding me, d'ye hear? Stop it, I tell you," cried Stacy, wriggling from their grasp, red of face, an expression of great indignation in his eyes.

"Did you swallow a bone?" queried Ned.

"Bone nothing."

"Then, please tell us the cause of all this unseemly disturbance. Your table manners are about the worst I ever saw, Stacy Brown."

"Water," gasped Stacy.

"Here," twinkled Walter, passing the pail.

"What's the matter with the water?" demanded Ned.

"Somebody's been putting old eggs in it. I believe you did that, Ned Rector, just to tease me."

Ned did not understand what the fat boy meant.

"Here, pass that pail. Is there anything the matter with that water, Walt? You got it."

"I think it is thoroughly good, wholesome water," replied Walter, holding his head low over his plate that they might not observe his amusement.

"Ugh!" exclaimed Ned, after tasting the liquid. He hurled the remaining contents of the cup full into the camp-fire.

"I told you so," nodded Stacy solemnly. "It's eggs and they weren't laid yesterday, either."

"You're right. Walt, where did you get that awful stuff?"

Tad and Walter were both drinking deeply of the liquid and apparently enjoying it.

"From the spring," gasped Walter, placing his cup on the ground.

"Don't drink that stuff. It'll make you all sick," commanded Ned.

"Don't be silly. That water is all right," laughed Tad.

"All right? Call that all right?" demanded Ned.

"Call that all right?" echoed Chunky.

"Of course it is. It is mineral water - sulphur water," spilling over his clothes the contents of the cup that he was carrying to his lips. Walter was laughing so that he finally let go of the cup itself and rolled over on his side, shouting with merriment.

"You can have it," announced Ned firmly.

"Yes, all of it," added Chunky. "I'll take my eggs hard boiled after this."

"Drink it. It will do you good, Chunky," urged Tad.

"No, thank you. I wouldn't offer it to a mule."

"So I see," flung back Ned, with a malicious little grin appearing in the corners of his mouth. "But speaking of mules, I wonder if it has occurred to anyone that our mules might be wanting a drink, too."

"Haven't they had any water to-day?" asked Tad.

"Haven't seen them drink since we left Springfield."

"Why, of course they have had water every day. They could not live without it."

"If they're like me they could - if they had to drink egg water," grumbled Stacy amid a loud laugh from his companions.

"I'll attend to them right after supper," decided Tad. "But just now we had better talk over our own situation. It is plain that something has happened to the Professor. How much longer will our provisions last, Ned?"

"Well, on a rough guess, I should say not beyond to-morrow."

"Then I should say in the first place that it would be wise to put the outfit on half rations beginning to-morrow morning -"

"No, no, no," protested Chunky, springing up and waving his plate excitedly.

"You won't have anything before you know it, young man," warned Ned.

"Yes, but we may have to stay here a week, if the Professor does not return. I do not see what good it will be to begin starving us until it is necessary," objected Walter.

"It will be necessary to-morrow," replied Tad.

"And after to-morrow what?"

"I shall hope to have some provisions here by that time, Ned."

Ned Rector laughed.

"Yes, I can almost see it now. How do you propose to get them, may I ask?"

"Go after them."

"Where?" queried Walter.

"Red Star mining camp. It cannot be so very far from here."

"Going to drag the mules after you?" asked Ned in a half sarcastic tone.

"No, I'm going on foot."

"What!" exclaimed the boys in one voice.

"You heard me. If Professor Zepplin has not returned by to-morrow morning I'm off for assistance and a fresh supply of food."

"And leave us here alone?" cried Chunky.

"Don't you see, fellows," continued Tad, "the Professor undoubtedly is in a worse fix than we are. He may wander about the mountains until he starves. I've simply got to stir somebody up to start out hunting for him. By remaining here we are only getting deeper into trouble. Don't you understand that?"

"Yes," admitted Ned. "But, then, why not let us all go with you?"

"Yes, that's the idea," interjected Walter.

"No, that is not good judgment."

"Why not?"

"In the first place some one must remain here to watch our outfit. We don't want to lose anything more than we have."

The boys nodded.

"Secondly, the Professor might possibly find his way back here, and the chances are he would lose himself again trying to find us."

"That's so," chorused the boys.

"And thirdly, as the Professor says, I can get along a lot faster alone than if you are all with me."

"Fellows, I understand why our friend Tad Butler wears a hat a size and a half larger than any of us - his head's bigger. Yes, you're right, Tad."

"Yes, yes," shouted Walter and Stacy, "that's the reason."

"And don't I get all I want to eat until he-he - until Tad gets back?"

"That depends upon how much you want. Judging from past experience, I should say you wouldn't," replied Ned.

"But what will happen to us if you get lost, Tad?"

"Yes, yes, that's what I want to know?" questioned Ned.

"I'll see that I don't."

"How?"

"This time I am going to blaze every tree I pass, with my hunting knife. It will enable me to get back if I fail to find the way, and it also will serve to guide the men here, if I find any to return with me."

"I take off my hat to you," exclaimed Ned.

"How many eggs have we left, Ned?"

"A dozen hard boiled ones, I think."

"Then I'll take three. I'll eat one for breakfast and carry the other two with me. That will leave three apiece for the rest of you."

"Oh, take a drink of water from that - that spring and save your egg till you need it," suggested Chunky.

"I'm going to start early in the morning, so I guess I'll turn in now. Remember, you are not to leave this place till I get back - that is, unless the Professor should return in the meantime."

"We promise," answered the lads together.

After putting the camp in shape for the night and attending to the mules the boys turned in and slept the night through without further incident.

Next morning when they turned out, Tad Butler had gone. On a piece of paper pinned to a tree they found a note reading: "I'm off, fellows. Bye."

CHAPTER XII

ALL GONE BUT TWO

"Well," grunted Ned Rector, as he served the meager breakfast, "at this rate there soon will be nothing left of the Pony Rider Boys except the skeletons of two mules."

Chunky, solemn-visaged, was munching his hard boiled egg slowly, in an effort to make it last as long as possible.

"This all I get to eat to-day?"

"Eat? No, certainly not. I'm going to cook all the rest of the day for you. Let's see, you shall have a porter-house steak, fried potatoes, some nice fresh salad and a soup plate of ice cream and -"

"And a finger bowl," finished Chunky, without the suspicion of a smile.

"Yes, with egg water in it," added Ned.

It was the longest day they had ever put in. There was no difference of opinion on that point when the day was ended. They had hoped to hear from Tad before nightfall. He did not return, however, and they had little hopes of his doing so now that the darkness was coming on.

There was no merriment in the camp that night. By dint of careful management they had saved enough out of their supplies to give them a light breakfast on the following morning, After that they had no idea how they should manage, providing no assistance came to them.

The mules were the only indifferent ones in the party. They munched the green leaves contentedly, sleeping when they were not eating. Near the middle of the night one of the animals set up a loud braying which brought the boys from their cots in quick alarm. At first they could not imagine what it was. They tumbled out, shouting to each other.

"What is it, Indians?" cried Stacy, dancing about in his pajamas.

"No, it's nothing but a mule with an overloaded stomach," answered Ned turning back to his tent growling his disgust.

"Wish it wouldn't dream quite so loudly," grumbled Chunky.

When morning came, and still no tidings from either the Professor or Tad, the boys began to realize the seriousness of their position.

"Something's got to be done, fellows," announced Ned Rector.

"I wonder if we could not shoot some game,"

suggested Walter.

"That's a good idea. But, is there any game here?"

"I heard an owl last night," said Stacy.

"We haven't got down to owls yet. We may when we get hungry enough," returned Ned. "I think I'll take my rifle and go out gunning."

"Do you think the Professor would like you to do that?" questioned Walter.

"I am sure he would not wish us to starve. There must be some kind of game in these mountains that's fit to eat. I'll shoot almost anything that comes along."

"Don't you get lost, now," cautioned Walter.

"No danger. And I'll bring back something to eat, you take my word for that."

Ned, with rifle thrown over his left arm, stepped boldly from the camp, heading west, reasoning that this direction would take him into the heart of the mountains where he would be more likely to find game.

An hour passed; then they heard a gun.

"He's shot something," exulted Walter.

"At something, you mean," corrected Chunky.

A second shot followed quickly on the first, then a third one.

"Guess you're right, Chunky," smiled Walter.

Later on they heard three more shots.

"That sounded a long way off," mused Walter. "I'm afraid he is getting too far from camp."

Chunky nodded thoughtfully.

"He thinks he can shoot, but he can't. I wish I had a fish line. I'd go down to the river in the gorge there and see if I couldn't catch a fish. Maybe I can fix up something that will -"

"No, you don't, Stacy Brown. You stay right here. You would get lost before you got out of sight of the camp. I don't want to be left alone here, with nothing but a pair of long-eared mules for company."

Stacy shrugged his shoulders and began idly cutting his name in the bark of a tree with his knife.

"Funny we haven't heard Ned shoot in some time," said Walter after a long interval of silence. "He must be working his way back. Think so?"

"Nope," answered Stacy, still engaged with the knife.

"You don't? Why not."

"Hasn't got any more shells, that's why."

"I don't understand."

"He shot six times, didn't he?"

"Let's see - yes, I believe he did."

"Well, that's all the bullets he had in the gun. He'll have to throw stones if he sees anything else to shoot at."

A startled expression appeared on Walter Perkins's face.

"You're right, Chunky. But why don't he come back, then?"

"Lost, I guess," replied Stacy, not appearing to be in the least disturbed by his own announcement.

Walter started up in alarm.

"You don't - you don't think -"

"No, I'm just guessing."

"If - if Ned should get lost, too, it would be awful."

Stacy nodded indifferently, Walter meanwhile pacing restlessly back and forth.

The lad's face wore a troubled look. With the Professor and all his companions save Stacy, gone; with no food left in camp, Walter Perkins had reason to feel alarmed.

Chunky, however, whittled on undisturbed.

"Are you hungry, Chunky?" asked Walter, pausing in his walk, later on.

Stacy nodded.

The day had worn along well into the afternoon and neither of the boys had had anything to eat since early morning. Their appetites were beginning to assert themselves.

"I'm going to get some mineral water. It surely will help some. Come on, it won't hurt you."

Stacy turned a pair of resentful eyes on his companion.

"No egg water for me. I'll starve first," he answered, with more spirit than usual.

While Walter went to the spring to help himself to the sulphur water, Stacy stood off to view his artistic work on the bark of the tree.

"Guess - guess they'll know I've been here, anyway," he mumbled.

"That's real good stuff," announced Walter, as he returned. "I do not feel nearly so hungry as I did before. Better try some."

Stacy made no reply to the suggestion.

When twilight came on, Walter Perkins was more alarmed than ever. There could be no doubt now that Ned Rector had missed his way. Stacy remained unmoved. He bedded down the mules. When he returned from this duty he carried something bright in one hand. Walter's eyes caught it at once.

"What have you there?" he demanded.

"Can of orange marmalade," replied Chunky, with a twinkle. "Guess it must have been dropped out when we unloaded the pack. Good thing there's only two of us to eat it."

CHAPTER XIII

WINNING THROUGH PLUCK

Tad Butler had left the camp at daybreak. He started off at a slow trot which he kept up over the rough, uneven ground until some time after sunrise, all the time keeping the mountain gorge in sight so that he might not lose his way.

He had eaten no breakfast, having simply taken a cup of sulphur water, believing that he could make better time on an empty stomach. However, he now sat down and munched on one of the three hard boiled eggs he had taken with him.

"Guess it will be a good thing to rest for half an hour," he said to himself. This he did, by stretching flat on his back, after having finished his scanty breakfast.

Sharp on the half hour by his watch, Tad sprang up, greatly refreshed. Leaning well forward he dropped into a long, easy lope, which carried him over the ground rapidly. Hard as nails and spurred on by the need of his companions, the lad pushed on and on, blazing his trail as he went, not feeling any fatigue to speak of. Now and then he would pause for a few moments to make sure that he was not straying from the river gorge, which occasional rocks and foliage hid from his view.

At noon Tad sat down and ate another egg.

"I must be getting near the place," he mused.

Still there was no trace of human habitation. There remained nothing for him to do save to push on, which he did stubbornly.

When the sun went down he seemed no nearer to the object of his search than when he had set out at daybreak. The lad, after looking about, came upon a tree which he climbed in order to get an unobstructed view of the country. He argued that camp-fires would be lighted for the evening meal. Not a sign of smoke could he discover anywhere.

Tad's heart sank.

"I've got to stay out all night," he muttered. "If I were sure of finding some one in the morning I wouldn't mind."

There remaining about two hours before dark, he decided to push on as long as he could see. So he trotted on resolutely until the shadows fell so densely about his path that he could no longer find his way.

Tad reluctantly halted and after selecting a suitable place, gathered wood for a camp-fire. Water there was none, so he had to do without it while he ate his last egg.

Then he lay down to sleep, refusing to allow himself to think very long at a time of his lonely position.

Late that night, the boy awakened, finding the moon shining brightly.

He got up and looked about him. The camp-fire had died out. The light of the moon was so strong that he could make out the surroundings almost as well as in daylight.

"I may as well go on," he decided. "Perhaps I'll get somewhere in time for breakfast. If I don't I surely will have no breakfast, for I haven't a scrap of food left."

So he trudged on. He did not run this time, for a little more care than he had been exercising was now necessary to avoid pitfalls in the shadows cast by rock and tree.

Daylight came, but still the weary boy kept on his way. Hungry? Yes, Tad was actually faint for want of food. He tried the experiment of chewing some leaves that he knew were harmless. At first this gave him some relief. After a little it made him sick, so he did not try the experiment again. He feared he was going to give out.

Toward eleven o'clock the boy came out upon a rise of ground overlooking a long slope. He rubbed his eyes almost unbelievingly.

Halfway down the slope was a shack and off beyond it stood a man with his back turned toward him.

Tad uttered a shout of joy and began leaping down the incline. The man down there, startled by the cry, wheeled suddenly and descrying the figure of Tad Butler racing toward him, ran to his cabin, appearing a moment later with a rifle in his hands.

A moment more a second man dashed out, he too carrying a gun. Both men stood facing the lad, until, when he got near enough, they discovered that it was a boy; then they laughed and lowered their weapons.

Tad fairly staggered up to them.

"Act as if ye'd seen a ghost, young feller. What's the excitement about?" demanded the first of the two men.

Tad explained as best he could between breaths, at which the men laughed more heartily than ever.

"I want something to eat first of all. I'm half starved," he told them.

"Sorry, younker, but we ain't got more'n enough for ourselves. It's a long ways to where we kin git more."

"But I am willing to pay you for it. I must have food right now," protested Tad.

"So must we."

"Who are you?" demanded Tad indignantly. "I didn't suppose there was a man mean enough to refuse a boy at least a piece of bread when that boy was starving."

"We're prospecting. I reckon we know our business best. Ye can't get any chuck out of this outfit."

"Then tell me where the Red Star Mine is. I've got to get there at once."

"She's nigh onto fifteen miles off thar -"

"Why, that's the direction I came from," exclaimed the lad.

"Sure. Ye must have dodged it. Did ye pass the Ruby Mounting?"

"I don't know. Where is it?" asked Tad Butler.

"You'd know if ye saw it once. It's a peak that looks red when the sun shines on it."

"No, I didn't pass the place. Tell me how I can get to the mining camp, even if you won't let me have anything to eat," begged the boy. "My companions will starve before I can get back unless I get help to them soon."

"Got a compass?"

"Yes."

"Then lay yer course north by northwest three p'ints and ye'll hit the Red Star plumb in the eye - if ye don't miss it," and the miner laughed coarsely. "Know anybody there?"

"Mr. Munson, Richard Munson."

"Dick Munson, eh?" returned the man, with increasing interest.

"I'll be going now. Much obliged for directing me, at least," said Tad, turning away and starting with compass in hand.

The men said something to each other in a low tone, but Tad paid no attention to them, hurrying away as fast as his weary limbs would carry him.

"Hey, young feller, come back here."

Tad did so reluctantly.

"Sorry we can't give ye anything to eat. My pardner and I reckon though that ye can milk the goat if ye want to."

"The goat?"

"Yep. The goat's our milk wagon - she gives milk for the outfit."

At first he thought they were joking, but Tad suddenly realized that the men were in earnest.

"I - I never milked a goat," he replied hesitatingly.

"Well, if yer hungry enough ye'll try."

"Where is the goat?"

"Oh, I dunno. Browsing hereabouts, I reckon. Look her up if ye want to. We ain't got time."

"Thank you. I'll try."

"Mebby you'll find her over in that little draw there to the left," suggested the miner.

Tad sought the draw and after some search came upon the goat rather unexpectedly. The animal gazed at him suspiciously and moved off when he spoke to her.

Tad coaxed without avail, until finally with a handful of green leaves, that he had pulled from a branch above his head, he managed to excite the animal's interest. While she was nibbling at his offering, Tad patted her and after a time managed to quiet her sufficiently to enable him to get around to one side.

He had milked cows, but this was his first experience at milking a goat. As a result the lad went about his task rather awkwardly. Holding his cup with the left hand and using the right, he soon filled the cup, gulping down the contents greedily.

"Gracious, that tastes good!" gasped the boy. "I never knew goat's milk was anything like that. I suppose I can take all I want."

He helped himself to another and still another cupful, until he felt that he could hold no more.

"Thank you, Mrs. Goat," he soothed, patting the animal, while she in turn rubbed her nose against his sleeve as much as to say, "You're welcome. Help yourself if you wish any more."

"No, thank you, I think I have plenty, but you shall have some more green leaves."

Tad pulled down branch after branch which he piled up in front of the goat, and which she attacked with vigorous nibbles and tugs.

Very much refreshed, the boy ran back to the miners' shack.

"How much do I owe you?" he asked.

"Don't owe us nuthin'."

"Well, here is twenty-five cents. I thank you very much," replied the lad, laying the money down in front of the door of the shack, because the miner refused to reach out his hand for it.

"You're welcome, kid. Mebby we might squeeze out a chunk of bread after all."

"I think I have had plenty. I do not feel hungry now," he smiled. "How far is it to the Red Star the way you have directed me?"

"As the eagle flies, 'bout twelve miles. You'll make it in fifteen, cause you'll have to go around a draw that you can't get through. When you get round the draw just come back till ye git on yer course again," directed the miner.

"Thank you. Good-bye. Hope I have a chance to return the favor some time," smiled Tad, swinging his hand in parting salute, as he started with renewed courage.

The fifteen miles of rough traveling did not discourage him in the least. He reasoned that he ought to reach the mining camp by four or five o'clock that afternoon. That would be in time for him to start back with food for the other boys, whom he had left in camp.

"My, but I'll bet Chunky is a walking skeleton by this time," smiled Tad, as the thought of his companion's appetite came humorously into his mind.

Talking to himself to keep up his courage, consulting his compass frequently, that he might not stray from the course in the least, the lad hurried on. Reaching the draw that the miners had described, he recognized it at once, worked his way around it and came back. He might have shortened the journey had he but known how to work out his course by the compass. Tad realized this. He told himself that he could not afford to try any experiment, however.

His judgment was verified, when, shortly after four o'clock he was gratified by sighting several pillars of black smoke.

"That's the place. I've hit it!" exulted the lad, breaking into a sharp trot, which he increased until he was running at top speed.

With clothes in a sad state of disorder, eyes red and sunken, Tad Butler burst into the Red Star mining camp. His sudden entrance caused the few people about to pause and gaze at him in astonishment.

"Where's Mr. Munson - Mr. Richard Munson? I must see him at once," he asked of one of these.

"He ain't here."

"What! Not here?"

"No."

"Then where is he? I must find him," expostulated the lad.

"Reckon you'll have a long run, then. He's gone over to

the Mears mines. That's a good twenty miles from here, I reckon."

Tad groaned in his disappointment, and sitting down on a rock, buried his head in his hands.

CHAPTER XIV

RESCUE PARTIES ON THE TRAIL

"Who is in charge in his place? There must be some one that I can talk to," demanded the lad, starting to his feet.

"Might see Tom Phipps, the assistant superintendent."

"Where is he? Tell me quickly."

"See that shack over there?"

"Yes."

"Well, if he ain't there, he's somewhere else."

"Thank you," said Tad, unheeding the fling.

Tad started for the shack at top speed. He burst into the place, which proved to be office and sleeping place as well, without even thinking to knock, so excited was he.

A young man, who sat studying a map, glanced up in surprise.

"Mr. Phipps - Mr. Thomas Phipps, I want," said Tad.

"I am he."

"I beg your pardon for my seeming rudeness, sir, but I'm in an awful hurry."

"So I have observed," smiled the young man. "What is it - is there something I can do for you?"

"Indeed there is. I had hoped to find Mr. Munson, as he would know who I am. You do not, but I am going to ask a very great favor of you -"

"Perhaps I may know, if you will tell me," smiled Phipps.

"I am Tad Butler, one of the Pony Rider Boys, and we're in an awful fix."

"Shake," nodded the assistant superintendent, extending his hand. "Of course I know about you. Dick has told me about your trips this summer and he's been expecting you almost any time now. When he left this morning he charged me to be on the lookout for you. Where's the rest of your party?"

"I'm afraid most of them are in trouble."

"Tell me about it."

Tad related in detail all that occurred since they left Springfield, not omitting the sudden disappearance of the Indian, nor the loss of the ponies.

"So you've been hit too, eh? You are not the only ones who have lost stock. It's getting to be a common thing in this part of the country. Nor do they confine their depredations to stealing horses. They help themselves liberally to whatever they happen to want. It's never seen again. They have some secret method of smuggling their plunder from the range that we can't discover," continued Phipps breezily.

"I am most concerned just now with getting food to my companions and having some one start out for the Professor," urged Tad.

"Yes, I'm thinking that over. There are not many ponies in camp here. We had more, but the same thing happened to them that did to yours," said the young miner. "I think Munson is planning to make a round-up of the country with the idea of breaking up the band. You stay here while I go out and see what I can do about it. By the way, have you had anything to eat?" asked Phipps suddenly.

Tad told him honestly what he had had.

"Three eggs and a drink of nanny goat milk, eh? Not much to travel more than thirty miles on. Can you cook?"

"After a fashion," admitted Tad.

"Then get to work. There's bacon. You'll find bread and butter in the large tin box there. Help yourself. I would cook it for you only I would rather get things going for your friends," said Phipps cordially.

Tad protested that he could help himself and urged the miner to make all haste possible. After the latter had left him, the lad lost no time in starting the fire and in a few moments had bacon sizzling in the spider and the coffee pot steaming. He found some cold potatoes which he fried in the grease of the bacon.

"Don't that smell good!" exclaimed Tad, as the odor of the cooking drifted up to his nostrils. "If it tastes half as good as it smells I'll have the meal of my life."

He was not disappointed. Tad ate and ate, yet he was wise enough to restrain himself and chew his food well, knowing full well that he would have to submit himself to a still further test of endurance before he could call his work done.

The lad was still eating when Tom Phipps returned.

"What luck?" cried Tad anxiously.

"It's all right. I've rounded up enough ponies for the party. I have called six of the miners from work. They are men who know the mountains. The cook in the chuck house is preparing food for you to take back with you - that is if you intend to go -"

"Of course I do," spoke up Tad quickly.

"I think it will be best for the whole party to return with you to the place where your friends are camped. From that point they can start on the trail. They'll find the Professor. No doubt about that. After you all get back we will talk with you about the loss of your stock. Perhaps your experience may help us to land the band. I hope so."

"Can - can your men find their way in the dark?"

"I should say they could. Some of them know now

from my description just where your camp is. Don't worry about that. Here they come now."

The miners, leading an extra pony for Tad, rode up at that moment. When they glanced at the slight, boyish figure of Tad Butler they were of the opinion that he had best remain at the mining camp. They did not believe him hardy enough to stand the grilling journey that lay before them.

They changed their minds before they had been out of camp an hour. Tad rode well up with the leader, sitting in his saddle like a veteran, taking obstructions in their path with jumps that some of the party balked at and rode around.

"Say, kid, where'd you learn to hit a saddle like that?" called one.

"Does my riding please you?" inquired Tad.

"I should say it did. You are no tenderfoot."

Though the party rode rapidly, the hour was late when they reached the vicinity of the Pony Rider Boys camp. Having approached the place from another direction, Tad did not know where he was.

"It must be somewhere hereabouts," decided the leader. "Can't you remember whether it was to the north or the south of this?"

"Which way is the gorge?" asked Tad.

"That way. Lays right the other side of those rocks."

Tad considered for a moment.

"Wait," he said, a sudden idea coming to him. "I do not remember this particular spot, but when I left the camp I blazed trees all along so I could find my way back. If there are any marks on the trees here, I made them."

The men leaped from their ponies and began examining the trees, from the cliff back several rods. Not a sign of fresh blazing were they able to discover.

"There's nothing here," announced the leader.

"Then I didn't go this way," answered Tad, with a note of finality in his tone.

"We are too far to the north, boys. Turn around and follow the canyon."

This they did until they had proceeded for something like half an hour, when the leader of the rescue party decided to get down again and examine the trees.

"Here's a blaze. Is that yours, kid?" he exclaimed.

Tad examined the mark on the tree carefully, having first lighted a match to aid him.

"Yes, yes; I did that."

"Then we've gone by the place. There can't be anybody there or we would have seen the camp-fire."

"They must be there! Let's go back over the ground!" exclaimed Tad.

The men turned about without another word. After a few moments had passed Tad began calling loudly.

Soon a shout just ahead of them told the party that at last they had found that which they were in search of.

Tad uttered a glad cry.

"Where are you?"

"Here," answered the voice of Stacy Brown.

Tad put spurs to his pony and dashed up to where he thought the voice had come from.

"Where are the rest of the boys?"

"Got anything to eat?" asked Chunky, rousing himself to full wakefulness.

"Yes, plenty. But where's Ned and Walter? Are they asleep?" insisted Tad Butler half fearfully.

"I don't know."

"What do you mean?"

"Ned went off to hunt some game because we didn't have anything to eat. He hasn't come back. Walt got crazy about it and I guess he went out to look for him, though he didn't tell me he was going to -"

"What time was that?" interrupted Tad.

"When Ned went away?"

"No, when did Walter leave?"

"I don't know. It was somewhere about sundown when I saw him last."

"Which way do you think he went?"

"That way, I guess," replied Chunky, pointing.

By this time the men had lighted the fire.

"Give that boy something to eat right now," commanded the leader the moment he set eyes on Stacy. "He's half starved. He can hardly stand."

They opened the package of food at once, giving the once fat boy a little at a time at first and compelling him to eat slowly.

"Then there is not one of them here but Chunky," muttered Tad.

"No - nobody but me and the mules," answered Stacy quickly.

No one thought of laughing.

"Are we not going out to look for the others now?" asked Tad.

"Yes, I reckon we might as well," decided the leader. "We'll leave your friend here till morning. One of our men will remain here with him. At daylight they will start for the Red Star. If anything has been heard there of the folks we are looking for, they can then send word back to us so we don't spend the rest of our lives hunting for them."

His plan seemed a logical one to Tad. The party was to spread out, covering a large area, literally dragging the mountains with a human net, it being agreed that when one made a discovery he was to inform the others by shooting twice into the air.

After having received their instructions the men quickly rode away. The moon had come out, lighting the way and making their journey much easier.

Stacy gave no further heed to the miner who had been left in charge of him, and promptly went to sleep on a full stomach. He had not experienced that agreeable sensation for some time.

The night was well advanced when two sharp reports from the south told the searchers that some of their party had gained tidings of the absent ones.

Each man wheeled sharply about and raced for the camp as rapidly as the rough trail would permit, arriving there about the time their leader rode in with Walter Perkins. He had found the lad less than half a mile from camp. Beyond being very badly frightened, Walter seemed none the worse for his experience. Instead of having followed the direction in which he had started, Walter had gradually worn around to the north until finally he was headed back toward their original starting point.

In a short time he realized that he was lost. He called loudly for help, but as there was no one to hear his cries, he had at last thrown himself down on the ground in despair to wait for morning.

It was there that the leader of the rescue party had stumbled upon him, Walter having heard and answered his hail.

"That's one. Spread out again, boys. We'll rope the rest of the youngsters before morning. They can't be far away. The Professor, as they call him, has a horse, and there's no telling where he is by this time."

But the task they had set for themselves this time, was not quite so easy of accomplishment.

CHAPTER XV

THE ROUND UP

Some miles from the camp the searchers next morning came upon an abandoned camp where there had been a fire and where, from the bones found there, they decided some one had eaten a rabbit.

"We're on the trail," said the leader. "We'll get him yet."

An hour later one of the men reported that he had picked up a repeating rifle with the magazine empty. When Tad joined them later, he identified the weapon as having been the one used by Ned Rector.

The course he was taking, if followed, would eventually take him out of the mountains into the open country. Perhaps through some instinct, the boy understood this and was seeking to gain the open where he would soon get food and directions for continuing his journey.

They found no other trace of the one they were looking for, however.

All that day and the next they drew the net slowly over that portion of the Ozark range that cut through the southwestern part of the state.

"I guess we shall have to give it up," confided the leader to Tad.

"Oh, no, we can't do that," objected the lad hastily. "We simply must find Ned and the Professor."

"If you can show me the way how or where, I wish you would then. We are only a few miles from the mining camp. I'll wager a jack rabbit couldn't have gotten through our lines, so we'd have been pretty likely to have rounded up a man on a pony or a boy on foot. Don't you think so?"

Tad was forced to admit that this was true.

"It's my idea that neither of them is in the range now, at all. If they are, they're below the Red Star - gone by the place entirely."

"That may be, but I do not see how it is possible."

"You went by her, didn't you?"

Tad colored.

"I guess so. But it was different in my case."

"Ah, that's it. It's different with them, too. If it wasn't, we would have found them long before this."

"Then you are going to give it up? Is that what you mean?"

"Don't see as there is anything else we can do. If we

don't come across them this afternoon, we won't at all. See, there's the Ruby Mountain already."

"The Ruby Mountain! I've heard of that. What a peculiar formation it is. Almost blood red in spots. What is it - isn't there some superstition about the rock?"

"Well, you might call it that. There are those who declare they have seen strange lights appear on the face of the rock after dark."

"Have you?" queried Tad.

"Well, that's another story," laughed the leader.

"What makes it look so red?"

"That's the quality of the rock. It is red only when the sun or bright moonlight is shining on it. Isn't really red, you see."

Tad did not see, but his mind was too full of his own troubles to permit him to interest it deeply in the subject of the Ruby Mountain.

Continuing on their journey, the searchers eventually rode into the Red Star camp. By this time the entire camp was interested in what it was pleased to call "the man hunt." Somehow they were unable to free their minds of the idea that the disappearance of the members of the Pony Rider party was due to the mysterious band that had been terrorizing that part of the country for a long time.

Tom Phipps, assistant superintendent of the mine, had

awaited the return of his rescue party with an impatience that he made no effort to conceal. He met them, mounted on his pony, as they entered the mine property. At first he was inclined to make the men turn about and go over the ground again, but after learning from the leader of the party the precautions they had taken, he decided that further search to the north would be futile.

What to do next he did not know, and in the absence of Mr. Munson, who had not yet returned, he was considering sending another party out to cover the territory south of the mining camp.

Stacy Brown had come in with his guide and the mules, and having satisfied his appetite, was in as good humor as usual. If he worried about the disappearance of his companions, he kept his trouble well to himself. Nevertheless he was waiting for Tad and the rescue party when they rode in.

"Hello, Chunky, any news?" called Tad on espying him.

Stacy shook his head.

"Have you any?" asked Chunky.

"No. We found where Ned had been, but we didn't see anything of him."

"That's too bad."

"Yes, you do seem to feel sad over it. I believe they are all right, however. Mr. McCormick, who has charge of this party, thinks so too. He believes they have succeeded in getting out of the mountains."

"So do I," cut in Tom Phipps. "Otherwise you could not have missed them."

"Yes, sir. But what would you advise doing now?"

"Should we hear nothing from them by morning I'll start a party for the open country to the west, and send another through the mountains south of here. I do not believe there will be much use in doing so to-night. Come over to my shack, you and your friend Brown, and we will talk the matter over while we are having our supper."

"Thank you. I guess I am pretty hungry. Has Mr. Munson returned?"

"No. I cannot imagine what is keeping him."

Turning his pony over to Mr. McCormick, Tad and Chunky followed the young mining engineer to his one-roomed cabin where the host had prepared an appetizing meal.

It was Tad's second meal in the place. This time, however, he found himself too much disturbed to eat heartily. His appetite seemed to leave him all at once.

"As I was saying just after you arrived," began Mr. Phipps -

"Hark! What was that?"

Tad raised a hand for silence.

"I heard nothing."

"It was somebody shouting, I am sure," answered Tad in a voice of tense expectancy. "Yes, there it is again."

"You're right," answered the miner, springing up and hurrying to the door.

The shouting now became general all up and down the street.

"What is it?" asked Tad.

"I don't know. Seems to be a party coming into the camp. It's Munson, that's who it is. There are two people with him on foot. I can't make them out in the twilight. Come on, we'll hurry down and find out what the uproar is about."

Instinctively Tad and Tom Phipps set off at a jog-trot, followed more leisurely by Stacy Brown.

Tad soon observed something familiar in the movements of the two figures who were walking beside the superintendent's pony, and in a moment Tad made out through the gloom the well-known form of Professor Zepplin.

"There they are! There they are!" he shouted. "They've got back. Hurrah!"

"Rah!" echoed Stacy Brown, flirting one hand lazily.

The meeting was a joyous one for all concerned.

"All hands come over to my shack," glowed Tom

Phipps. "I want to hear about this mystery. Thought you were riding a pony, Professor Zepplin?"

"He was," laughed Dick Munson. "Some other people wanted the animal more than he did and helped themselves."

At this point, Walter, who was staying in another cabin, having heard the noise, had hurried over and joined the little party.

"Now let us hear all about it," urged Phipps, after all had gathered in his shack.

"There is not much to tell," smiled the Professor. "I did exactly what I had been warning my young men against. I lost myself. Then the next thing that happened, I lost my pony."

"How?" interrupted Mr. Phipps.

"I don't know."

"Stolen," nodded Dick Munson.

"Same old game," muttered Phipps. "Yes, what next?"

"Then in a most miraculous way I found Master Ned. I had gone to sleep, worn out and discouraged, not caring much whether I got back or not, the way I felt then. Along toward morning I woke up. I thought I had heard something. I listened, and then all at once realized that some one was snoring not far from me."

"And it wasn't Chunky this time," cut in Walter Perkins.

"Chunky doesn't snore on an empty stomach," laughed Tad.

"I called out, 'Hello, who's there?' The snorer woke up calling out something that I could not catch."

"Who was it?" asked Stacy in a hurry to learn what the Professor was getting at.

"Well, when he woke up he said his name was Ned Rector and that he was lost."

The Professor smiled grimly as the boys shouted with laughter, in which Tom Phipps joined. Even the rugged face of the superintendent relaxed into a broad smile.

"Yes, it was I," nodded Ned. "We had been sleeping within a rod of each other nearly all night and didn't know it. I had stumbled along after the Professor got to sleep. In the darkness of course I did not see him, and in his sound sleep he did not hear me."

"That's the funniest mix-up I ever heard of," chuckled young Mr. Phipps. "What did you do for food?"

"Master Ned, it seems, had shot two rabbits which he intended to take back to our camp. When he found that he too was lost, he built a fire and cooked them. What he did not need at once he wrapped up in his handkerchief and carried along with him -"

"Yes, we found the remnants of the jack rabbits," Tad informed them. "We picked up your rifle later, as well."

"Good," brightened Ned. "I had to throw it away. I had

about all I could do to carry myself."

"Well, the rabbits saved us from starvation."

"Yes, but how did you happen to find Dick Munson, or he to find you?" queried Phipps.

"We wandered out of the mountains and lost ourselves in the foothills. How we got so far south I do not know. This morning we saw a horseman and shouted until we attracted his attention. The horseman proved to be the very man we wanted to see - Mr. Richard Munson himself."

"I - I am the only one who didn't fall in," piped Stacy, which caused everyone to laugh.

"We heard you shooting," said Walter. "I wish we might have had some of that rabbit meat. We nearly starved up there."

"Yes, let's hear how you boys got along," spoke up Ned. "We have told you all about our experiences. Now we want to know about yours."

Tad related in detail all that occurred to them since the Professor left them in pursuit of the elusive camp-fire. The Professor's eyes glowed appreciatively upon learning of Tad Butler's heroic tramp over nearly forty miles of rough mountain trail in the desperate effort to find food for his starving companions as well as help to rescue them from their perilous position.

But Munson, while complimenting Tad, was more deeply interested in the loss of their stock, about which occurrence he asked many questions.

"If we had a few men with your courage and resourcefulness we should soon put a stop to this wholesale thieving," he said.

"I'm going to find my pony before I leave this place, Mr. Munson," announced Tad firmly. "At least I am going to try pretty hard -"

A knock on the door of the shack cut short what he was going to say.

"McCormick reports that two ponies are missing from number two section," said a voice outside the door.

CHAPTER XVI

THE VOICE IN THE ROCK

"The thieves are getting bold!" was Dick Munson's comment.

"Seems to me they not only are getting, but have been for some time," laughed the Professor. "The condition of my feet proves that."

The Number 2 section to which the superintendent's informant had referred, was a quarry mine, off among the mountains in the vicinity of the red rock that had attracted Tad's attention as they neared the camp. He made a sudden resolve to visit the place on the following day.

Borrowing a pony next morning, and without telling anyone where he was going, Tad rode away with the Ruby Mountain as his destination. The trail was an easy one to follow and, besides, he had so recently been over it that he would be able to find his way there and back.

Just why he felt such a keen interest in the place the lad did not know. Perhaps it was that the miners had thrown such an air of mystery about it in speaking of the red rock. Aside from its color there was nothing about the pile of stone to distinguish it from almost any other rocky formation in the Ozark range, unless it were the slight resemblance that it bore to the form of a church. The lad had observed this the first time he saw it.

After riding around the pile, Tad dismounted, and, tethering his pony, proceeded to examine the place more carefully.

The rock was rough and uneven, with little spires running up here and there. The lowest of these was a considerable distance from the ground.

"I'd like to climb up there if I knew how," decided the boy, looking for an advantageous place to make the attempt.

"I have it. I know what I'll do. I'll rope the rock."

Tad laughed gayly at the thought as he ran back to where he had tethered the pony in the shrubbery. Tom Phipps had seen to it that the outfit was fully equipped, having added a lariat, because Tad had jokingly inquired where this necessary equipment was.

"Glad I happened to think of that. I'll never ride out without a rope again, even if it's up and down Main Street in Chillicothe."

Fetching the rawhide rope he skilfully cast it up and over the pinnacle of rock nearest to him. It was now a comparatively easy matter to climb by going hand over hand up the rope and bracing his feet against the side of the rock at the same time.

Once having reached the point where the rope had been fastened, the rest of the way was less rough.

The lad sat down to look about him, noting that the formation was a peculiar one, and that the reddish shade of the rock disappeared when one came into close contact with it.

"Why, it's just a plain, ordinary pile of stone," laughed Tad. "The idea that there could be anything mysterious about it! I'll climb up to the top and see if there is anything more interesting there."

There were frequent narrow crevices that the young explorer discovered on the way up. These appeared to reach down to a considerable depth, but having no weight to attach to the end of his rope he could not sound the depth with any degree of certainty. One of these crevices was large enough to admit his body.

The place fascinated him.

"I'm coming out here prepared to go down in that hole and investigate it," he said to himself. "I'll bring the boys - no, I won't either. I'll explore it all myself and maybe I'll find out something."

The lad was coiling his rope, preparing to descend when a low chuckle caused him to pause in sudden surprise. Startled, the boy looked about him. He was alone as he had been before.

"That's strange. I was sure I heard some one. Sounded as if it were right here beside me. I must have been wrong of course. Believe I'm losing my grit. After all the shaking up my nerves have had on this trip -"

"Hello!"

This time there could be no doubt. It was a human voice beyond all question.

"Hello," answered Tad, when, an instant later, he had in a measure mastered his surprise. "Where are you?"

"Guess."

"I can't. I am not a good hand at guessing."

Getting to his feet the lad began searching about, peering into crevices, looking over the edge of the cliff, becoming more and more perplexed and mystified as the moments passed.

"No, I can't find you. Come out and show yourself, whoever you are," he commanded, with some impatience.

A low, mocking laugh answered Tad's irritated command, yet the owner of the voice still remained hidden.

"Who are you, anyway? I know you are a girl, but -"

"But what?" tantalized the voice.

"That's all I know about it, and all I shall at the present rate. Come on, it's not fair to expect me to talk with you when I can't see you -"

"Aren't you afraid of ghosts, boy -"

"Ghosts!"

Tad uttered the word in a startled voice.

"Wha - what ghosts?"

"Yes."

"No, I'm not," he answered sharply. "But if it were night I think I'd run. Pshaw! you're no more ghost than I am. You're just a girl and I am going to find out where you are right now."

Acting upon his resolution, Tad began searching for the owner of the voice again. But when he had crawled to one side of the rock, the voice appeared to be on the other, where he had just been.

After a time Tad gave it up. He no longer heard the mysterious voice, so he clambered down, and after examining the rock from the ground once more, mounted his pony for return to camp.

Arriving there, his companions wanted to know where he had been, but Tad managed to evade their question without giving them a direct answer.

He was determined to return on the following day, when he would go about finding the owner of the mysterious voice in a different way.

When Tom Phipps came in from work, Tad drew him aside at the first opportunity.

"I've been over to the Ruby Mountain to-day, but please don't tell anyone."

"Saw something, did you?" laughed the assistant superintendent.

"No, that's the trouble. I didn't."

"What happened then?"

"I did not see, but I heard." Tad then related all that had occurred on his visit to the strange mountain.

Phipps did not laugh. He remained silent and thoughtful for some moments.

"That's strange. A miner prospecting there came back with a similar story a few months ago. Nobody believed him, though many strange things are said to have happened in the vicinity of that rock."

"What?"

"That's the trouble. One cannot get them to tell what they saw. You have come the nearest to doing so."

"Only I just missed it by about a mile," laughed Tad. "But you do not think it's - how shall I say it?"

Phipps bent a keen glance on the young man. "You mean through any supernatural agency?"

Tad nodded.

"That's what I wanted to say, but didn't know just how to put it."

"No, I am too practical to believe any such trash as that. My idea is that some one of a humorous turn of mind is trying to play tricks on people. You say it was a girl's voice?"

"Yes."

"That's strange. I'm going to look into that."

"Let's you and I go over there together to to-morrow, then," urged Tad enthusiastically.

"I'll do it - that is, if there is nothing on hand to detain me. I'll let you know later whether it will be possible or not."

"Very well. I have been thinking - wondering whether -"

Tad hesitated.

"Wondering what?"

"Whether that rock has anything to do with so many horses and things being stolen in the range."

Tom Phipps laughed heartily.

"I never thought of it in that light. Don't see how a rock could possibly have any connection with it. Guess we shall have to look for something more human than a pile of stone."

It was decided, therefore, that on the morrow the two should visit the Ruby Mountain, when they would make a careful examination of the place in an effort to solve the mystery.

But they were destined to delay this trip for some time, and to pass through some exciting experiences before they solved the mystery of the Ruby Mountain.

CHAPTER XVII

WHEN THE DARK HORSE WON

"Professor, Mr. Munson says there's going to be a roping contest and horse race near here, this afternoon. May we go over to see it?" asked Ned Rector early on the following morning.

"Well, I don't know about that. Haven't you boys had enough straying from home for a time?"

"We can get some one to go with us and show us the way," urged Walter.

"Yes, let the lads go," said Mr. Munson, coming up at that moment.

"Where is this place?" asked the Professor.

"At Jessup's ranch. It is about ten miles to the southeast of here, just outside the foothills of the range."

"I am afraid they would never find the way there and back," objected Professor Zepplin, shaking his head doubtfully.

"That is easily taken care of. I will have some one go with them. Why not go yourself?"

"I? No, thank you, not without a guide. I have had quite enough experience in trying to find my way about in these mountains," laughed the Professor.

"Then I'll have Tom Phipps go with you. I understand the boys are fond of anything in the horse line, and they usually have a great time over at Jessup's. He is a cattle man and, besides his own men, cowboys from neighboring ranches for twenty miles around ride in to take part."

"But, we have no ponies."

"I think we can arrange that all right. Here, Tom, I want you."

Mr. Phipps approached the little group, the superintendent, informing him in a few words of the plan he had in mind.

"Of course I'll go with them," smiled Phipps. "I'll be glad of the chance to get out in the open once more. We had better get started pretty soon if we are going."

"How about it, Professor?" queried Mr. Munson.

"I do not object if Mr. Phipps accompanies them."

"Hooray!" shouted the boys.

"Wish we had our own ponies," added Ned.

"So do I," chorused the others.

"You will come along, won't you, Professor?" urged Walter.

"No, I think not. I've had quite enough for a time. Think I will remain and study the geological formations of the strata hereabouts."

"There's plenty of it to occupy you for some time," laughed Tom. "The most important zinc mines in the world are strung along this range. And besides, there's lead enough hereabouts to supply the armies of the world if they were all engaged in active warfare."

Arrangements were quickly made for the trip to Jessup's, and the boys, full of anticipations for a pleasant day in the saddle, donned their chaps and spurs, and began practising with their ropes, while the ponies were being saddled and made ready for the journey.

"Do we take our rifles, Professor?" asked Stacy.

"You do not," answered the Professor, with emphasis. "What do you think you will need with guns at a horse race?"

"I - I don't know but that we might meet some wild animals," stammered Stacy.

Everybody laughed.

"Why, there are no wild animals of any account here," laughed Tom.

"Nothing bigger than a jack rabbit," said Ned.

"And Ned Rector got all there was of them," added Walter.

Laughing and joking, the lads mounted their ponies and set off for a day's pleasure.

The entertainment at the ranch was scheduled for the afternoon, so they had plenty of time in which to make the journey. They arrived shortly before noon, just in time to see the preparations made for a barbecue. A large Texas steer had been chosen for the occasion and roasted in a pit, and they were making ready to serve it.

Stacy's eyes stuck out as he saw the cook with a knife almost as long as a sword, cutting off slices as large as a good-sized platter, and serving them on plates scarcely large enough to hold the pieces, without the latter being folded over.

The fat boy managed to get an early helping by pushing his way through the crowd of hungry men that had gathered about the savory roast. When there was anything to eat, Stacy Brown would always be found in the front rank.

Just as they got started with the meal, a volley of shots sounded up the valley and a band of half a dozen cowboys, yelling, whooping and shouting came racing down on the Jessup ranch.

With a wild "y-e-o-w!" they circled the roast ox, then bringing their ponies up sharply, threw themselves from their saddles and greedily attacked the portions that were quickly handed out to them.

This barbecue and day of sports was one looked forward to by the cowmen with keen anticipation. Two a year were given on the Jessup ranch, one after the midsummer round up, and another late in the fall.

"This is great," confided Tad to Tom Phipps, as the two seated themselves on the grass to eat the good things set before them.

"It seems so to me. I don't get out of the mountains very often. I wish I could ride the way you boys do. You ride very well."

"We have to. At first some of us came a few croppers," laughed Ned, who had overheard the conversation. "Chunky had the most trouble, his legs being so short that it's difficult for him to reach the stirrups."

"I fell off," interjected the fat boy.

"That's a habit of his," laughed Ned.

"I wonder if they would let us take part in some of the games this afternoon," inquired Tad.

"Why, of course they will. I'll speak to Mr. Jessup about it," answered Tom Phipps.

When the owner of the ranch passed them later on, Tom called him, and after introducing the boys to him, told the rancher what they desired to do.

Mr. Jessup looked the lads over critically.

"It's a pretty rough game, boys," he smiled. "But you look as if you were able to take care of yourselves. Of course you may go in for the fun if you want to. I'll tell the bunch."

"Thank you," said Tad, rising.

Mr. Jessup shouted to attract the attention of the noisy cowboys.

"Hey, fellows, we have a bunch of tenderfeet lads from the East with us to-day. They're taking a trip over the mountains and they want to know if they can join you in the fun this afternoon?"

"Sure!" roared the cowboys. "We'll give the tenderfeet all the fun they want."

Tad smiled appreciatively.

"Don't let them disturb you," warned Tom. "They mean all right."

"Yes, sir; I understand cowmen pretty well. Have spent quite a little time with them."

"I guess they are getting ready for something."

"Line up for the hurdle race!" shouted the ranch foreman, who was acting as master of ceremonies. "Half mile down and back with a hurdle every quarter!"

"Here's where you see some real fun," announced Mr. Jessup, nodding significantly to Tad and Tom Phipps. "Are you boys going into this?"

"Guess we might as well. Will these ponies take hurdles, Mr. Phipps?"

"You try them and see. Every one trained down to the ground."

"That's not the way I want to go," laughed Tad. "I want

to stay above it while I'm riding."

Ned Rector already was tightening his saddle girths preparatory to entering, so Tad hurried to his own mount to get ready for the contest.

When the contestants had finally lined up, the Pony Rider Boys were surprised to observe that Stacy Brown had ridden down to the scratch with the others. He was sitting on his pony as solemn as an owl, industriously munching a sandwich that he had made for himself.

"You'll break your neck. You'd better keep out of this," advised Ned Rector.

"Better look out for your own neck," retorted Stacy. "Guess I know how to ride as well as the rest of you."

"All right, it's not my lookout. Remember I gave you good advice," was Ned's parting admonition.

Stacy's pony was a glossy black, the only one of that color among the contestants, and between pony and boy the cowmen were undecided as to which was the most conspicuous.

"At the second shot of the pistol you will start," announced the foreman. "All ready for the first?"

"Yes!" roared the impatient riders.

The foreman pulled the trigger and the ponies began to dance about.

Bang!

"Whoop-e-e-e!" yelled the riders, digging in the rowels of their spurs.

A dozen ponies fairly leaped into the air under the prod of spur and quirt. Away they dashed enveloped in a cloud of dust.

"They're off!" roared the crowd.

Stacy, still clinging to his sandwich, was well up with the leaders of the bunch when they got away. He was riding with elbows up to a level with his shoulders, one hand grasping reins and quirt, the other holding the sandwich to his mouth.

The spectators shouted with laughter at the sight.

"There goes somebody!" cried Walter.

One of the ponies had fouled the first hurdle and gone down, plowing the dust with its nose, while the cowboy made a fairly graceful dive through the air, landing on his head and shoulders. The riders directly behind him were obliged to hurdle pony and rider, which they did without mishap to either. Stacy, fortunately was ahead, else he too might have come a cropper.

This left a field of eleven, all of whom were bunched, their mounts almost rubbing sides. By this time the dust cloud was so dense that the spectators were able to make nothing at all of what was going on at the other end of the course.

"I hope the youngsters are all right," said Phipps a little anxiously, for the race was one of the roughest he had ever seen, and then the young miner was not much of a horseman, which made the contest seem much more hazardous to him than it really was.

"They're coming back," shouted a voice.

The turn had been made, but at the expense of two riders, whose mounts, less sure footed than the rest, had gone down in the sharp whirl for the home stretch.

The prize in this contest was to be a handsome telescope repeating rifle, and the rivalry for it was keen. The battle would be a stern one, and it was a foregone conclusion that the best horse would win.

Stacy Brown had not leaned far enough in at the turn, his saddle girth slipping a little as a result. He felt the saddle give a little beneath him, but did not realize what had happened until the pony had straightened away on the home stretch. The saddle then slipped still further under the weight of the rider.

Stacy threw almost the whole force of his weight on the right stirrup to offset the list of the saddle on the other side, where the stirrup had gone down too far for him to reach. And the first hurdle found the lad clinging desperately to the pony's mane with one hand, the jolt of the jump nearly dislocating his neck as the animal took it.

The youthful rider, finding himself safely over, uttered a series of shrill yells and began urging on the pony with quick, short encouraging blows of the quirt, though the blows were not heavy enough to hurt the tough little beast at all. It was used to much more serious treatment.

Somehow the animal seemed bent on doing its best, though the more it strove to reach the goal, the greater was the fat boy's torture.

Stacy Brown's grit was aroused. He seemed to have come into his own at last.

"They laughed at me," he muttered. "I'll show them that Chunky Brown isn't a tenderfoot. Even if I don't win the race, there will be some others who will finish after I get through." He was reasonably certain of this from his present position. "But I hope I don't fall in," he grinned.

By this time the dust caused by their first trip over the course, had settled so that the spectators were enabled to get a view of the last quarter of the race. And they all admitted, without exception, that it was a real race that they were watching.

Over the last hurdle went two ponies in beautiful curving leaps, ahead of all the others. With their cowboy riders they took the obstruction neck and neck. A full length behind them rode Stacy with the rest of the field strung out to his rear.

The spectators were able to identify the black now from their point of vantage, and Stacy could hear their cheers, though unaware that these were for him. Tad Butler, second to him in the race, was getting every ounce of speed from his pony that the animal possessed. Yet instead of feeling chagrin over the fact that his companion was out-footing him, Tad was elated.

"Go it, Chunky! Go it!" he encouraged.

"I am going," floated back to Tad faintly, causing him to laugh so heartily that he was nearly unhorsed when his pony rose to the hurdle.

As Stacy's mount cleared the last barrier, the fat boy fell forward on the pony's neck, which he grasped wildly, for the saddle in that final leap had, with disheartening suddeness, given way beneath him, slipping clear down under the animal's stomach.

Nothing daunted, Stacy, with his newly discovered grit, worked both spurs vigorously, eyes staring straight ahead of him over the head of his fleeing pony.

They were almost at the finish. Now the dust of the two cowboy leaders in the race did not smite him in the face as heretofore. He was too close up with them for that.

All at once the lad realized that he was gaining. Excitement among the spectators ran high. Observing his predicament and understanding full well the grit he was exhibiting, they were yelling like mad. Chunky began to yell also, uttering a series of shrill whoops, using voice and spurs incessantly, urging the pony to the goal.

The black pony, almost gray with the dust that had settled on his sleek, glossy coat, forged ahead in a noble sprint with head on a level with its back, nose reaching for the finish.

A roar of applause sounded in the fat boy's ears. Yells, cat calls and shrill whoops rent the air.

All at once a pistol barked, the black pony's feet

plowed the dust, bringing it to a sharp halt.

The suddenness of the movement caused Chunky's feet to rise straight up into the air. For a few brief seconds he was standing on his head on the pony's neck like a circus performer.

Then, as the animal lowered its head, the rider toppled over, still clinging to the neck of his mount. Such a chorus of laughter and shouting the Jessup ranch had never known before.

"How is it, Mr. Umpire?" piped Stacy, releasing one hand from the pony's neck and raising it questioningly.

"This isn't a baseball game, young fellow," jeered the foreman. "This is a hoss race and you've won it. The black wins and you get the rifle."

The grimy hand that the lad had held aloft still clung to the remnants of the roast sandwich that he had carried throughout race.

CHAPTER XVIII

TAD WINS A ROPING CONTEST

In their enthusiasm two of the ranchers hoisted Chunky to their shoulders and marched about singing. Others fell in behind them until fully half the spectators had joined the procession. Chunky leered down at his companions as he passed them and winked solemnly.

"I didn't suppose he could ride like that," marveled Tom Phipps.

"Neither did any of the rest of us," answered Walter.

"I never saw a more plucky piece of work in my life."

Tad came up to where they were, laughing heartily.

"Doesn't that beat all, Walt?"

"It certainly does."

"Our friends who were defeated do not seem to appreciate the humor of it, though," interjected the young engineer.

"No, not very sportsmanlike, is it? Who is that fellow with whom Chunky's competitors are talking?"

"Name is Cravath. Queer sort of a chap."

"Haven't I seen him about the Red Star?" asked Tad.

"Yes, no doubt. He is a checker at the mine. He and his wife and daughter have a cabin out near the Ruby Rock that you are so much interested in. I know very little about him -"

"Don't like his looks at all," decided Tad.

"No, I never warmed up to him very much myself. I understand he is not very popular among the men, either. But I guess that is because he wins their money in games of chance."

"A gambler?" questioned both boys in surprise.

"I wouldn't go far enough to say that. What are they going to do next here do you know?" asked the engineer, changing the subject.

"I believe it is to be a roping contest. That will be a lot of fun."

"You are not going in it, are you?"

"Of course. Why not? I don't know what they are going to rope, but I'll take my chance with the rest of them whatever it is. Guess I'll ride over and ask Mr. Jessup. I see him over there now."

Mr. Jessup when questioned informed the boy that it was to be a most realistic contest in which two men mounted were to try to rope each other. One of the rules of the contest was that the roper, when he caught his opponent, was to drop the lariat instantly so as not to pull his victim from the saddle.

As only two could meet for the prize it was decided that lots should be drawn from a hat. The two who drew slips of paper with the word "rope" written on them, were to have the honor of meeting in a test of skill.

The prize was a Mexican saddle, silver mounted, at which all the cowmen looked with covetous eyes.

"Think you want to take a chance for the saddle, boy?" asked Mr. Jessup.

"That I do," laughed Tad. "That's the saddle I want - I always have wanted one just like it. But I'm afraid I shall not get the opportunity to try for it."

"They are getting ready to draw. You had better go over," advised the rancher.

Tad found that they were not only getting ready, but that most of the men had already drawn. Only one "rope" slip had been taken from the hat, however, so there still was a chance.

He rode up to the foreman, who was holding the hat from which the drawing was being done.

"May I draw?" he asked.

"Do you know how to sling a rope, kid?"

"A little," answered Tad, with an embarrassed smile, for the cowmen were making uncomplimentary remarks about letting babies into a man's game. The boy's face burned, but he gave no heed to their ungentlemanly remarks.

The foreman held up the hat. Tad leaned over and drew from it a slip of paper.

"Next - who draws next?" demanded the foreman.

"If it will save you any trouble, I might suggest that it isn't necessary to draw further," Tad informed him, with the suspicion of a smile on his face.

"What's that?" asked the foreman sharply.

"I have the second slip," was the quiet reply.

The cowboys broke into loud exclamations of disapproval.

"Fair is fair, boys," warned Mr. Jessup. "You all had your chance and you lost."

"Yes, that's right," agreed the foreman. "You fellows will have to swallow your pills without making faces."

The man Cravath was now talking with the cowboy who had drawn the other slip. He was one of the men Chunky had won from, though Tad did not know it at the moment.

Tom Phipps pushing his way up to the lad informed him of this fact, and drawing Tad to one side whispered something to him.

"Is that so?"

"Yes, Cravath owns one of the ponies that came near winning the race. He is not a very good-natured man and I imagine they are putting up some plan to get even with you boys," warned Tom.

"I'm not afraid. They won't let them do anything unfair," said Tad. "Besides, I ought to be able to take care of myself, by this time, though I haven't been doing much with the rope of late. Is that chap an expert roper?"

"I couldn't say as to that. But he's big and strong -"

"Which doesn't count for very much in this sort of a contest," laughed the boy.

"Very well, you know best. But keep your eyes on him."

"Are you gentlemen ready to begin?" called the rancher.

"I must go now," said Tad hurriedly.

"Good-bye and good luck," breathed Mr. Phipps, as the lad rode away at the same time straightening out his rope which he allowed to drag behind his pony while he recoiled it, working it in his hands to limber the rawhide.

"It's a good rope," decided Tad.

The foreman halted them for final instructions.

"Now, gentlemen, understand that the rope must go over the head and be drawn taut, after which you are to let go of it. You are to take your places some distance apart - I'll place you - and start at the crack of the pistol, not before. Understand?"

Tad and the cowman opposed to him nodded, the latter with a sarcastic grin on his face.

The miner had lost the rifle which he coveted, and the cowboy did not propose to have the same luck in the case of the saddle, which was very valuable.

The cowboy had his rope in hand ready to begin, while Tad's had been hung over the saddle horn. The lad was sitting in his saddle easily, with a quiet smile on his face, and the spectators noted that he was not in the least nervous.

"I guess that boy knows his business," muttered Mr. Jessup, who had been observing him keenly. "At least he's got the pluck and will give a good account of himself, though he never will be able to win against a professional rope thrower."

In the meanwhile, the foreman had started to place the contestants. Tad had the sun in his eyes, but he made no protest, knowing that he could change his position as soon as they got the word to go.

"Are you ready?"

"All ready," answered Tad cheerfully.

"Yes," said the cowboy shortly.

Tad's rope was now held in his right hand. Both men put spurs to their mounts almost before the report of the revolver had died way. The ponies leaped forward and the two opponents rode straight at each other.

They passed at racing speed, neither making an attempt to cast.

No sooner had they cleared each other, however, than the cowboy pulled up his horse sharply, wheeled and dashed after the Pony Rider Boy. Tad, having foreseen the movement, had likewise stopped his mount, and turned about. But instead of spurring on, he stood still.

The cowboy had hoped to come up behind Tad and rope him as he raced away. He was slightly disconcerted when he noted Tad's position. But the smiling face of the boy angered him, and the cowman's rope squirmed through the air.

Tad ducked, allowing the lariat to shoot on over him. It fell harmlessly on the other side of his pony and a quick pressure of the spurs took boy and pony from under it.

With a "yip-yip" Tad rushed at his opponent. The latter had had no time to gather in his own lariat, but he began shortening it up intending to swing it from where it lay on the ground.

His opponent gave him no time for this.

Tad made a quick cast. The cowboy threw himself to one side, but the loop of the lariat that had been thrown true reached his broad sombrero, neatly snipping it from his head.

The spectators uttered a yell of approval. They shook

out their revolvers, sending a rattling volley up into the air.

Tad Butler had scored first.

His opponent was angered almost beyond control. That a mere boy could thus outwit him, which Tad had neatly done, was too much for his fiery temper.

With a growl of rage he drove his horse straight at the lad. It was plain that it was the fellow's intention to ride him down, which Tad circumvented by standing still until the man was nearly upon him, and then driving his pony out of the path of the oncoming horseman.

Each began a series of manoeuvres, the purpose of which was to place the rider behind his opponent, but each proved too wary to be caught in any such way.

The contest was growing hotter every moment, and the spectators were getting worked up to a high pitch of excitement. They had never seen a more interesting roping exhibition than this, and that a boy was one of the contestants gave their enthusiasm an added zest.

The two were, by this time, working far out on the field. Tad realized this and sought to get back nearer to their starting point. He did not, however, understand that his adversary had any object in getting so far away, though the man had a distinct purpose in so doing, as Tad eventually learned.

The foreman was shouting a warning to them, which Tad tried to heed, although his adversary prevented his doing so by blocking the way each time.

Whenever the opportunity presented itself the cowboy would bump his pony violently against the one that Tad Butler was riding, in an effort either to so jar the boy that he could rope him or else possibly to unhorse the lad.

"See here, you stop that!" shouted Tad after the third attempt. "What are you trying to do to me?"

"I'll show you, you freckle-faced tenderfoot!" yelled the cowboy, making a vicious rush. At the same time his rawhide shot out.

Tad narrowly missed being caught that time, and in turn the cowboy was nearly caught by Tad's loop. A lucky sweep of his arm brushed I the lariat away not a second too soon.

Tad observing that his adversary, who was about to cast again, had him at a dangerous advantage, threw himself down on the side of the pony's neck. Both animals were running almost neck and neck at the moment.

With a whoop the cowboy let go. His loop closed around the boy's ankle which from his position on the pony's side, was sticking well up in the air. Tad's opponent, suddenly braced his pony, while the boy's mount raced straight ahead.

The result of this move was that Tad Butler was torn from his saddle, fetching away the stirrup box on one side with him. He struck the ground violently, and for a moment lay still, while the cowboy sat grinning, making no effort to learn how badly his adversary was hurt.

The foreman and several others were rushing to the scene. By the time they reached it, Tad was scrambling to his feet.

"I roped the kid," announced the cowboy, as if it were all finally settled.

"You roped me by the foot," retorted Tad.

"Yes, that was a foul," said the foreman. "I saw it myself. How'd you come to do that, Bob?"

"Mistake," answered the cowboy, thus admitting that they were right.

Tad turned on him sharply.

"Did you say it was a mistake?" he asked with a world of meaning in his tone.

"We will award the prize to you, Butler," announced the owner of the ranch. "That's the usual way when a foul has been committed."

The cowboy glowered angrily.

"I couldn't think of accepting it, Mr. Jessup," answered Tad, straightening to his full height. "I'll go on with the contest, but he mustn't do that to me again or there will be trouble."

Some of them laughed at the boy's veiled threat.

"There certainly will be trouble," agreed Mr. Jessup - "trouble with me. I want you two to keep up the field further so we can see what is going on. Are you hurt, boy?"

"Shaken up a little that's all. Guess my saddle was worse used than I was."

The contestants lined up for another bout, amid the most intense excitement. So closely had the spectators gathered about them that the ropers had no room in which to work, and the foreman found it necessary to urge them back before giving the word to start.

The Pony Rider Boys could scarcely contain themselves. They, too, were worked up to a high pitch of excitement. But Tad Butler, dirty, with clothes torn and grimy, appeared to be the coolest one in the crowd. If he was angry no one would have imagined it from the pleasant expression of his face and almost laughing eyes.

"All ready! Go!"

They went at each other again, the cowboy ferociously - Tad easily, but keenly on the alert, narrowly watching every move of his opponent.

Round and round circled the pair, neither making an effort to cast for at least ten minutes, ducking, side stepping, or as near to this latter as a pony could get, and with movements much like those of boxers in a ring.

The crowd was offering advice and suggestions freely, but both men turned a deaf ear to all of this. Their whole beings were centered on the work in hand.

Once both men cast and their lariats locked, the

cowboy's loop having slipped over Tad's.

The foreman called a halt while he untied the tangle. The instant this had been accomplished, Tad drew in his with one hand, coiling it at the pony's side.

"Remember, I haven't called time," warned the foreman. "You are still roping."

Tad knew that, but he did not wish to take an unfair advantage.

The cowboy looked up with a startled expression on his face, but nodded and began hauling in his rope when he noted that Tad was making no move.

His rope was in.

"All ready," he said.

So was Tad. The boy's lariat shot gracefully through the air, landing neatly over the cowman's shoulders where it was quickly jerked taut before the other fully realized what had happened.

CHAPTER XIX

WRECKED IN AN ORE CAR

It was all the ranch owner could do to keep peace after Tad Butler had so cleverly outwitted his adversary in the rope throwing contest. Yet, though the defeated man was fairly beside himself with rage, the cowboys generally favored fair play.

Their companion had been beaten in a fair contest, principally because his opponent had been quicker witted.

Tad and Chunky, one bearing a rifle, the other a handsome saddle, were proud boys when they rode home with Tom Phipps and their companions that night. The Pony Rider Boys had carried away the real prizes of the cowboy meet. Chunky had few words. He was so filled with self-importance that he could only look his gratification. When part way home, however, he rode up beside Tad, and leaning from his saddle, whispered, "I didn't fall off, did I?"

The news of triumph spread about the mining camp quickly. When the miners learned that Cravath's pony and his man had been defeated, they shouted for joy. From that moment the Pony Rider Boys became persons of consequence in the Red Star mining camp.

It was suggested that evening that the whole party spend the next day in the mine. Tom Phipps had permission to devote the day to them if they wished to go underground.

"That will be fine," cried Tad, to which sentiment all the rest subscribed, except Stacy.

"I'm going hunting," he announced.

"Hunting? What for?" questioned Ned.

"Anything I can see."

"Then, I'm glad we are all going to spend the day underground. It will be about the only safe place around this part of the country."

"Remember, Chunky, that's a powerful weapon of yours and long range," warned Tad.

"And remember to watch out that you don't fall off your new saddle and break your neck," retorted the fat boy.

On the following morning the boys, with the exception of Stacy, reported at Tom Phipps's shack ready for the day's sight-seeing in the zinc mine far underground. The assistant superintendent had made ready a large basket of food, as the party was to dine in the mine.

Professor Zepplin was enthusiastic. It was an opportunity that he had much desired.

"I understand," he said, fixing Tom Phipps with a stern glance of inquiry, as they started for the mine, "that

Silurian species have been found in the limestones hereabouts. Also that others believed to be Cambrian have been discovered. Is this in accordance with your experience?"

"I think I understand to what you refer," answered Tom gravely. "I can't say that I am familiar with the species, however."

"If Chunky was here he would want to know if it were something to eat," laughed Ned. "I'm not very certain myself whether it is or not."

"You'll be wiser by-and-by," said Tad.

Entrance to the mine was gained through a shaft leading straight down for a great many feet. A windlass and bucket was employed to carry the miners up and down, while through another and larger shaft automatic buckets raised the zinc ore to the surface.

All of the party could not be accommodated in the passenger bucket at one time, so it was necessary to make two trips, Mr. Phipps returning with the vehicle to see that the rest of the boys got down safely.

Descending into the cool, damp darkness was a new experience for them. And while the sensations were not particularly pleasant, they agreed that it was the most interesting journey they ever had taken.

"How far down do we go?" asked Walter.

"About fifty feet," answered the miner. "Of course the mine is not that far underground all around. Some of the strata of rock we work lead almost to the surface in places."

"Why don't you begin at the top and work down then?" questioned Tad.

"Some of the mines do that. In this case it was deemed best to sink a shaft. Here we are."

From the darkness the boys had suddenly been plunged into a blinding glare of light. It was so intense that at first they were unable to see anything.

"Good gracious," blinked Ned. "This is brighter than the opera house at Chillicothe. It's enough to put a fellow's eyes out. What is it?"

"Electric lights," laughed Phipps. "We don't have many conveniences above ground, but down here we are right up-to-date, as you have observed."

"As I perhaps shall observe when I am able to get my eyes open once more," added Ned humorously.

"Why, the place is full of tunnels!" exclaimed Walter.

"Regular checker-board under ground," agreed Tad. "Where do all those tunnels go to?"

"Under where you have been tramping since you have been in camp."

"To the Ruby Mountain?" inquired Tad meaningly.

"Yes, most probably that far, or pretty close to it, I should say; but I have never made a measurement with that in view, so that I am unable to give you a definite answer. We should have to bore through some pretty solid rock to get under the little red mountain, I'm inclined to think."

"I'd like to go over that way."

"All right, we will visit that part of the drift later," replied Mr. Phipps.

What Tad's motive might have been in wishing to get under the Ruby Mountain, perhaps he himself did not know. But he did know that somehow he felt that before leaving the mining camp he would solve the mystery of the place.

They first followed the drifts to the west where here and there a dull distant report told them the miners were blasting out the rocks with dynamite. After being broken up into large chunks the ore was placed on little cars and run along tracks to the hoisting apparatus from where it was quickly shot to the surface.

It was a busy scene that the Pony Rider Boys found - a different world from the one they had just left above them.

"Do these mines ever blow up or catch fire?" asked Walter a bit apprehensively.

"No, we have no fires of any consequence. We have never had an explosion and I trust we never shall," answered the assistant superintendent gravely. "You see there is not the same danger in this sort of place that you find in a coal mine. I would prefer to work digging out dynamite to mining coal."

"Dynamite? Do you keep much of it down here?" interrupted the Professor.

"Oh, yes, we have to. There is enough down here at this moment to more than blow up the Ruby Mountain. The greater part of it is stored in what is known as the Ozark drift, the drift running to the southeast. I'll show it to you when we go that way."

Now they were nearing the more active operations and the metallic click of the steam drills filled the air as they bored their way through the solid rock, necessitating the raising of voices that the boys might make themselves heard.

"Would you like to take a ride in one little cars?" asked Mr. Phipps.

The boys were quite certain that they would enjoy such a trip.

"Pile into the next car, then. We'll send it through without any ore this time. There would not be room if we were to load the car. I think it will be a novel experience for you."

And Tom Phipps smiled significantly.

Directing the switch man to shift the car back to the return track, the mining engineer told the lads to climb in and sit down on the floor, which they did promptly.

Only the tops of their heads projected above the sides of the ore car.

"Under no circumstances must any of you straighten

up unless you wish to get your heads smashed."

"Why, there is plenty of room for our heads here," replied Ned. "We could stand up and yet have some to spare."

"Right here, yes. We shall go through some places that you would not want to stand through, I imagine."

"Are you ready?"

"Yes."

Tom Phipps climbed over into the car.

"All right, Jim," he called.

Immediately the car began to move and in a few moments had attained a high rate of speed.

"Now, boys, remember your heads," cautioned their guide.

Instinctively each crouched lower as their vehicle was all at once plunged into sudden darkness. Drops of water now and then spattered down on their bare heads. The noise of the car in the dark was deafening. The sound was as if many ore cars instead of one were crashing through the dark tunnel. The lads experienced a strange thrill when the realization came to them with its full force, that they were shooting through the earth, far beneath the surface at the speed of an express train.

"Why don't you have lights in here?" asked one of the passengers.

"Not necessary," said Mr. Phipps. "It is seldom that anyone has occasion to go through this tunnel - practically never unless something happens to a car in here. There are lights along that may be turned on if necessary, but it would be a needless expense to keep them going all the time -"

"What's that loud noise?" asked Tad.

His ears had caught a booming roar that was a new note in the terrifying sounds of the underworld through which they were traveling.

The boys started uneasily.

"It's water," shouted the guide. "A cataract in an underground water course. These courses have cut channels all through the limestone rocks in the Ozark Uplift."

This somewhat calmed the nerves of the lads, though not wholly so. Faster and faster rolled the car and louder and louder grew the roar of the cataract.

"Are we almost out of here?" demanded Walter uneasily.

"Yes. We shall be clear of it in five or six minutes now. You notice that we strike little grades occasionally, which cause the car to slow down considerably and for that reason the journey seems longer than it really is."

"If we have slowed down at any time I have failed to observe it," laughed Tad.

"What if we should jump the track in here?" suddenly

suggested Ned.

"But we won't," answered the guide. "We -"

A grinding, crunching sound cut short his words. The car appeared to pause and tremble throughout the length of its frame; then followed a deafening crash, accompanied by the sound of breaking timbers and splintering wood.

A deep silence, broken only by the roar of the cataract, settled over the scene. The ore car lay a broken, twisted, hopeless wreck.

CHAPTER XX

A MESSAGE THAT THRILLED

Out of the silence came the voice of Ned Rector.

"Help, I'm pinned down," he groaned. "Get me out of this awful hole."

"I'm coming as soon as I can get free of what's on top of me," answered Tad. "Is everybody else all right? W-a-l-t! Mr. Phi-ipp-s!"

Tad struggled desperately and in a brief time succeeded in freeing himself. What had happened to the guide and to Walter he did not dare to think.

First upon getting clear of the obstruction that pinned him down, he rushed to Ned Rector and succeeded in releasing him without great difficulty. Neither boy was hurt much.

"Where's the other two?" cried Tad in a voice of anxiety.

"I don't know. Don't know where I am myself," groaned Ned.

"Hurry, help me find them."

Together the boys groped about in the black tunnel.

"I've got one," called Ned.

"Which one?"

"I don't know. Yes, yes, it's Walt. He's breathing. What shall I do?"

"Drag him over to one side. I've got Mr. Phipps here. I'll have him over there in a minute."

Tad began tugging, with hands under the shoulders of the guide, understanding instinctively that he must get him where they could work over him and try to bring him back to consciousness.

Something whizzed by in the darkness, the rush of air nearly knocking both boys over, and leaving them trying to catch their breaths.

"Wh - what's that?" gasped Ned.

"I - I don't know," answered Tad. "Yes, I do too. It - it was a car returning on the other track for a load of ore."

The lad's knees went weak under him when it came to him that he had only a second before dragged the unconscious figure of the young engineer from that very track.

Now still another sound startled them. It was a roar heavier than any that they had heard before, and as near as they could tell, it was from the direction that they had come.

"Hurry, Ned!" shouted Tad Butler fairly electrified by the thought that suddenly flashed over him.

"What is it? What is it?"

"I - I don't know, but I think it's a car of ore rushing down the grade toward us."

"We're dead ones, then!" cried Ned.

"Be quick, Ned! Grab Walt and run as you never ran before!

"On, on! Keep to your right so you don't get on the return track. Oh, Hurry!"

Tad had already gotten into action. Once more grasping the guide by the arms, the lad ran backward with his heavy burden, with almost marvelous speed under the circumstances.

He was none too soon. Back of him he could hear Ned stumbling over rails and ties with his burden. Then came the heart-rending crash.

The car of ore had plunged into the wreck of their empty car, hurling rocks in all directions. Had they remained where they had been, there would have been none left to tell the story of their experiences.

"I guess it's all over," shouted Ned. "But, there will be more, soon, and some of them may hit us."

In obedience to Tad's command, Ned dragged Walter along a few rods further, where on a curve both boys laid down their burdens.

Tom Phipps under the rough treatment that he had received was stirring and making an effort to sit up. Tad helped him along by slapping him vigorously between the shoulders. Ned was shaking Walter almost savagely.

"Wake up, Walt! Wake up! What's the matter with you?"

Walter groaned.

By this time Tom Phipps had partially pulled himself together.

Tad's heart leaped with joy.

"Walt will be all right in a minute, I guess," Ned informed him.

"And so will Mr. Phipps."

"Where am I?" asked the young engineer.

"We've had an accident, Mr. Phipps," replied Tad. "How do you feel?"

"As if I had been put through the ore mill. Did we have a smash?"

"I should say we did?"

"Who's hurt?"

"Walter was knocked out too, but he is coming round now. Ned thinks the boy is not hurt very badly."

"No, I'm half scared to death, but I'm all right otherwise," answered Walter for himself.

"Which track are we on?" demanded Phipps suddenly, trying to locate his position.

"Our own. You nearly got run over on the other. I pulled you off just in time."

"I'll thank you later. There must be a cross cut near here. If we can find it we'll be able to get to a point where I can telephone them to hold back the cars. They'll fill the tunnel before they know anything has happened, if I don't get word to them at once."

"I should think they would miss the cars."

"They should," answered the engineer. "Is your friend able to walk?"

"How about it, Walter?" called Tad.

"Yes, I can run if it will take me out of this terrible place any sooner."

"Then we'll run," decided Tom Phipps. "I must have gotten an awful hit on my right leg, for I can scarcely bear my weight upon it."

"Shall I rub it for you?" asked Tad.

"No, we haven't time. We must look for that cross cut, which leads into the number eleven drift. Keep to your right, boys. We are safe here now, but not on the other track."

"I know that," answered Tad. He shuddered as he recalled the black, projectile-like object that had whisked by him just after he had pulled Mr. Phipps from the return track.

There was still another reason why the assistant superintendent was so filled with anxiety to reach a place where he could notify the terminals to stop the cars. He did not confide this to his young friends, not wishing to disturb them any more than they had been.

All hands started on a trot, now stumbling, now falling, but without a single murmur, or protest.

"You are a nervy bunch of boys. Never saw anything to equal you," gasped the engineer. "I can't forgive myself for getting you into this wretched mix-up."

"You never mind us. We're all right," answered Tad brightly. "I'm sorry you got knocked out so."

"Here's the cross cut," cried the miner. He had paused and was cautiously feeling his way along the wet, slippery wall.

The boys breathed a sigh of relief.

"Now run as if the Indians were after you. I'm in a bigger hurry than I ever have been in my life."

And run they did.

The boys had no idea what Tom Phipps's reasons were for urging such haste upon them, but they knew they must be urgent ones.

Tad found himself wondering what new peril might be facing them. He decided that the assistant superintendent must be seeking to protect the company's property by stopping the sending of more cars through the tunnel. Yet, if this were so, why had the guide urged them to such haste.

"No," said Tad to himself, "it's something that we don't know anything about. But unless I am greatly mistaken we are going to find out pretty soon."

In this the boy was right. They were to find out what it was that Tom Phipps feared, and in a manner that they would not soon forget.

The narrow cut through which they were now rushing was little higher than their heads, and was very narrow, so that by raising their elbows they could barely touch the sides and keep themselves in the middle of the passage way.

"Look out for a turn just ahead," warned Phipps. "After that it is straight away."

The turn which they made a few seconds later, Tad imagined, led back toward the place where the car had started from. But they came to the end of the passage abruptly.

They caught a faint click, and instantly they were surrounded by dazzling light. As soon as they became used to the brightness they discovered that they were in a sort of chamber which looked as if it had been worn out by constant and long action of water.

Instantly upon switching on the light, the young

engineer sprang to a telephone on the wall. Tad observed that the wires from it followed out into the passage through which they had entered.

The assistant superintendent was telephoning now, and the lads listened intently.

"Hello, hello!" called Phipps in an impatient voice. "Yes, who's this? Acomb? Say, Acomb, there's been a wreck on the number one track just west of here. Two cars smashed, one loaded the other carrying myself and some young men, guests of the company. Don't let any more through until the wreck is cleared away. Send an empty along with the wrecking crew so we can get out. What's that?"

Tom Phipps shuffled his feet about nervously on the stone floor.

"Hurry then, hurry! Yes, we're all here, but hurry!"

The boys instinctively drew near. They imagined that they could hear each other's hearts beat, so tense was the silence.

He turned halfway around to glance at the boys.

"Is it anything serious?" asked Ned in a strained voice.

"I hope not. I can't tell you just yet. We shall know in a minute... Well, send some one for him," he snapped, answering something the man at the other end of the line had said to him. "Hello, hello! That you, Bob? Did Acomb tell you of our predicament? Yes. What I wanted to say was don't for goodness' sake send out the red car while the line is blocked."

"The red car," repeated Ned and Tad in one voice. Neither knew what it meant, but impressed them just the same.

"What, gone? gone?" groaned Phipps. "Are you sure? How long ago? Ten minutes? Shut off the current! Quick! I hope so."

The assistant superintendent hung up the telephone deliberately and turned toward them.

The boys observed that his face was white and drawn.

"What, what is it?" asked Tad.

"There's a car of dynamite coming through the tunnel on the number two track," announced the young engineer calmly, thrusting both hands deep into his trousers pockets.

CHAPTER XXI

IMPRISONED IN A MINE

"That - that's the track that the empty cars go back on, is it not?" asked Tad, after an interval of tense silence.

"Yes."

"The wreck was on the other track."

Tom Phipps nodded.

"Then what harm can the red car, as you call it, do?" interrupted Ned Rector.

"That remains to be seen. The chances are that the number two track was blocked when the car of ore was spilled out."

"Which means?" questioned Tad.

"That there may be another collision," smiled the assistant superintendent. His was a wan smile, however, and failed to enliven the Pony Rider Boys.

"Will the dynamite explode?" asked Walter half fearfully.

"Probably not. I hope not. But you can't tell anything about these high explosives. They're very freaky. All we can do will be to remain here and wait for the car either to stop somewhere after the power has been turned off or to rip its way through the wreck we just left. At any rate we are safe in here."

The boys breathed a sigh of relief.

"Then, there is no danger to us?" asked Ned Rector.

"The danger is minimized."

"How far are we from where we started?"

"Probably a couple of miles."

"My! the Professor will be half scared to death when he hears what a fix we are in," half laughed Ned.

"The foreman, Mr. Acomb, said he would telephone to the other end of the drift telling them we were all right and not to worry about us," said Phipps. This relieved the boys' minds of one source of worry.

"Hark!" cautioned the young engineer.

The lads ceased their talking instantly and listened with straining ears.

"What is it?" breathed Tad.

"It's a car going through the tunnel."

"Is - is it the red car?"

"I don't know. It's a gravity car - traveling along down grade by its own weight, so it must be on track two."

"What can we do?" asked Ned.

"Not a thing, my boy, only keep cool. It will not help matters any to get excited."

"We are not!" replied Ned firmly. Each of the other two boys protested that they had never been less excited, which brought an approving smile from their guide, who was filled with admiration for the plucky lads. The fact is, his admiration had been steadily growing since he had seen their achievements from the time Tad Butler had first staggered into the Red Star mining camp a few days before.

"I guess the car is going through safely. I am glad -"

Tom Phipps did not finish the sentence. He was interrupted in a way that shook all the speech out of him, as it did from the rest of the party.

There occurred a sudden sharp tremor of the rocks about them; then the stones beneath their feet seemed to heave up and down. Their little universe was being turned topsy-turvy, it seemed to them.

At the first tremor, the Pony Rider Boys were thrown prone upon their faces on the rocky floor, partially stunned by the sudden shock. A distant boom, like the report of a cannon sounded in their ears, then all at once a terrifying rending of the rocks about them, accompanied by loud crashes.

"Are you all right?" shouted Mr. Phipps after the

deadening effect of the shock had passed.

"I'm all right," returned Ned Rector. "Can't anything kill me now. I'm proof against bullets, wrecks and earthquakes."

"Was that an earthquake?" questioned Walter weakly.

"Dynamite. The red car exploded when it was wrecked," explained the mining engineer. "That was what I feared. Is Master Tad hurt?"

"No, he's all right, I guess," answered Tad for himself. "All the lights have gone out. Can't we turn them on again?"

"I'm afraid not. The wires undoubtedly have been torn and twisted apart in many places. There will be no more light in this drift for some time to come, I reckon."

"Think anyone was killed?" asked Walter apprehensively.

"Oh, no. There was no one near the explosion, except ourselves, and luckily we are safe and sound. I'll try the telephone."

Mr. Phipps spun the handle of the telephone, but without result.

"Like the lights, it's dead," he said.

"What was that crashing noise in here? Was that what did it?" questioned Tad.

The miner struck a match.

"Look!" he exclaimed.

In the center of the chamber was a heap of rocks, weighing probably a ton or more. These had been wrenched from the roof of the place and dropped into the room where Phipps and the lads were waiting.

"Somehow, I'm feeling a goneness under my belt," spoke up Ned. "Let's get out of here."

"My goneness is in my knees," Walter Perkins informed them.

"Either place is bad enough," returned Ned.

"Do you think it safe for us to leave here now?" asked Tad.

"I have been waiting until I thought it was," answered the guide. "Of course, I have no means of knowing how much the explosion has loosened the rocks further out, near where the blast was fired."

"That's so," agreed the boys.

"We may have to face still other dangers, but I think we had better make a start. I am not sure that these rocks over our heads are any too secure, either. Have you boys any matches?"

"Yes, I have some," replied Tad.

"I'll use mine first, then. We'll need all we have before we get out into the car tunnel," said Tom. "Are you getting hungry?"

"To tell the truth, I for one haven't had time to think about my appetite," laughed Ned.

"Yes, I guess our minds have been so full of other things that our stomachs have not had a chance to make their wants known," said Tad.

"How about you, Walt?"

"What I want most of anything in the world just at this minute, is to see daylight. Isn't night outside yet, is it?"

"No, it is only just past noon," the miner informed him.

"Always have a total eclipse of the sun down here," muttered Ned humorously, but no one paid any attention to his feeble joke.

"If you are ready we will be going now," announced their guide. "Fall in behind me and go very carefully. You are liable to stumble over fallen rocks and break some bones. That's almost as bad as being hit on the head by one, eh?"

"Well, hardly," laughed Ned. "I've got that experience coming to me still, and I'm in no hurry to meet it."

"Keep as far to the side of this chamber as possible," directed Mr. Phipps. He proceeded ahead of them, lighting the way with matches, which served to relieve the darkness a little, casting weird, flickering shadows on the damp walls and ceiling of the narrow passage.

To the miner's gratification, the tunnel appeared not to

have been harmed at all, not a stone having been jarred loose so far as he was able to observe.

"I guess we are in luck, boys," he said in a relieved tone. "All clear so far. We shall be out in the main tunnel in a few minutes now. There will be a car along to pick us up very shortly after we get there."

"Hurrah!" shouted the lads joyously, hurrying forward in their anxiety to be clear of the place as quickly as possible. "Can you see the end of the place?"

"No, not yet."

They had just rounded the bend in the tunnel and were heading for the exit into the main cut. Drawing near to it, they observed that Tom Phipps hesitated, then began picking his way along with more caution than before.

"Anything wrong?" asked Tad, who was close behind him.

"I don't know. Be careful. There's a lot of rubbish under foot ahead. I don't like the looks of it at all. Stand where you are."

After proceeding a few paces, their guide halted, holding a match high above his head. He turned toward them slowly.

"The rocks have caved in, boys. There's a solid wall in front of us."

"Which means," asked Tad hesitatingly.

"That we are imprisoned far under the surface," answered the miner impressively.

CHAPTER XXII

THE BOYS FACE A MYSTERY

"Then how are we going to get out?" asked Ned Rector as the guide's match went out.

"That depends upon how long it takes to dig us out," answered Mr. Phipps.

"Then they know we are here?" questioned Tad.

"Oh, yes. Luckily for us, they do."

"Will they have to dig far - is that pile between us and the railroad very thick?" stammered Ned.

"It looks so. Of course I am unable to say what has taken place on the other side of it. The entire main cross cut may have tumbled in for all I know."

"If it has, what then?" demanded Tad.

"It will take that much longer to get us out. That's all."

"How long?"

"Master Ned, I don't know. No one can answer that question. Perhaps hours - perhaps days," said

Tom solemnly.

"But we'd starve in that time," protested Walter.

"One can go without food much longer than one would imagine. People have fasted for more than a month, as you probably are aware. No, boys, they will get us out in time. The only thing that troubles me now is the air," said the engineer.

"What about it?"

"Well, we can't live without air, you know. It seems to be fairly fresh now, but how long it will continue that way there is no knowing. I'll examine the barrier, but keep back out of the way while I am doing so."

The young engineer climbed over the heap of broken rock in front of him, and made a careful inspection of the cave-in that had so effectually imprisoned them in the drift.

He found nothing to encourage him. The condition of the collapse was even worse than he had anticipated.

"Can you pace - measure off by taking a series of long steps?" he asked.

"Yes," replied Tad promptly.

"Then please go back to where the bend in the cut begins, and pace down to where I am."

Tad did so promptly, glad to be able to do something to occupy himself as well as to help relieve the tension for the others.

"Exactly forty paces," he informed Mr. Phipps.

"One hundred and twenty feet, eh?" The engineer made a brief calculation in his mind. "One hundred and twenty feet. H-m-m-m."

"Is it as bad as you thought?" questioned Tad.

"Worse."

"Tell me what you have found?"

"Only forty feet of cave-in between us and freedom. That's all."

"I should say that was enough," muttered the lad.

"Ample."

"Is there anything we can do, Mr. Phipps?" spoke up Ned.

"Not a thing. All any of us can do at present is to wait. Knowing we are here, they will lose no time in attempting to get us out. I wish the telephone were working so we might let them know we are all right. We might as well go back. I'll make a trip out here occasionally to learn if they are making any signals to us. They will do this as soon as they can get near enough to the obstruction to make themselves heard."

"Make signals - how?" questioned Ned.

"We use a code, a telegraph code. They will rap with a hammer then we'll answer them."

"But you have no hammer -"

"No, I'll use a rock to pound with if they get near enough. There's no hurry, however. It will be a long time before there's any occasion to communicate."

Turning back, Tom led the way through the passage to the large chamber which they had but recently left. Arriving there, he directed each of the lads to light a match at the same time so he could make a survey of the room to determine whether it were safe for them to remain there or not.

"See that hole up there?" he exclaimed.

"Yes, what is it?" asked Tad.

"It's a check. You see there must have been a weakness in the strata at that point - perhaps it had already started to check there, when the force of the explosion split it wide open. The opening is large enough to admit a man's body. Hold your lights down here while I examine this rubbish that has fallen through."

They did so, and Mr. Phipps dropping to his knees sorted over the stones and dirt that had fallen from above.

At a muttered exclamation from him, the lads crowded closer.

"Queer, very queer," he mused.

"What's queer?" asked Ned.

"Why, this stuff. It appears to be surface material

mixed with pieces of rock of about the same quality as that of which the Ruby Mountain is composed."

"I don't understand -"

"I mean that this material that has fallen in here did not all come out of the solid rock."

"What does that mean?" asked Ned.

"Perhaps nothing so far as we are concerned. I was thinking that if they could not blast through the drift, they might as a last resort, drill down through the surface from above and pierce this chamber."

"How could they locate our position close enough to do that?" asked Tad.

"That would not be difficult. From the maps of the mine Mr. Munson could work out our position as closely as a captain does that of his ship at sea."

It was a ray of hope which the boys grasped eagerly. They tried to forget that they were practically entombed many feet underground, and that days might elapse before they were rescued.

"I'll bet Chunky will hug himself with delight when he finds out what's happened," suggested Walter.

"Yes, he'll probably think it's very funny, our being bottled up or rather down in a corner underground," said Ned somewhat dolefully.

"I didn't mean that. He'll be glad he went hunting instead of coming along with us," corrected Walter.

"Yes, I guess he will," agreed Tad. "He'll have a right to congratulate himself that he has missed an opportunity to fall in."

The lads forgot their predicament for the moment in the laugh that followed.

"I wish we had a light," said one.

"We might build a fire. What's the matter with burning up our hats?" suggested Ned.

"No, we should be suffocated. Don't you know we are sealed up," objected Tad. "We don't want to make any additional trouble for ourselves."

"Yes," agreed the guide. "But it is peculiar that there is so much fresh air here. Now and then I can almost imagine I feel a draft, though I know that is not the case."

"Could we not get a draft through that large crack in the rocks up there?"

"I don't see how, Tad. There is nothing but solid rocks above it."

The lad stepped under the opening, holding up a finger which he had wet between his lips. For a full moment he stood poised like a statue while the other two boys lighted matches that they might the better see what he was doing.

"I don't care what you say, there is air coming from somewhere. There can be no doubt of it. I feel it plainly. Try it and see if you don't agree with me,

Mr. Phipps."

The engineer stepped up and went through the same process that the boy had gone through. He repeated the experiment twice more.

"You're right," he exclaimed, letting his hand drop to his side. "Your good sense is worth more than all my technical knowledge and training."

"The next question is to find out where the draft comes from. It must be from the outside somewhere," said Tad hopefully.

"Not necessarily, my boy. Of course it may be drawn down through crevices covering many feet of solid rock before reaching us. Then again, the air may come from some subterranean water course. As you know the mountains are full of them, channel upon channel, some high and broad enough to drive a coach and four through."

"Oh. I hoped -"

"Never mind regrets, boys. Wherever the air comes from makes little difference so long as it really is air. It is saving our lives."

"From what?" demanded Walter.

"From eventual suffocation. Were it not for that we would stand a good chance of dying before they were able to reach us."

The boys were thoughtful for a few moments.

"Hungry?" questioned the engineer.

"Somewhat," admitted Tad.

"We might be more so if we had a chance to think about it," added Ned.

"I've got a package of chewing gum here. Help yourself," offered Mr. Phipps.

The lads were not slow to do so, and in a moment were chewing industriously, laughing and talking at the same time.

"Beats all what a little thing will make a fellow forget his troubles," said Ned. "Now, I remember -"

"Hello, boy!"

"Who said that?" demanded Tad Butler springing up from the pile of rocks on which he had been sitting for some time.

"Said what?" snapped Ned. "I was talking when you interrupted me."

"I thought I heard somebody say 'hello,'" confirmed Mr. Phipps.

"So did I," added Walter.

"And I know they did," said Tad emphatically.

"Hello, boy!"

This time all sprang up, startled.

"Who's playing tricks?" shouted Ned.

"Heard it that time, did you?" asked Walter. "It wasn't I."

"Nor I," chorused Tad.

"Then it must have been Ned or myself," said Phipps. "I'm sure that I am no ventriloquist."

For the moment Phipps wondered if they were all losing their senses. He had heard of men, imprisoned under similar circumstances, imagining they heard voices.

Tad Butler, however, knew that imagination had played no part in this voice. He had heard the voice before. He informed his companions of this fact.

"Heard it before? Where?" exclaimed Ned.

"On top of the Ruby Mountain yesterday," answered the boy.

CHAPTER XXIII

IN THE RUBY MOUNTAIN

Tom Phipps nodded. He recalled his conversation with Tad upon the other's upon his return from his visit to the Ruby Mountain, and the lad's description of the mysterious voice he had heard there. Mr. Phipps did not give very serious consideration to that part of the boy's story at the time. Now, however, he was startled beyond words.

All of them were startled. To hear a strange voice many feet down under the ground, when all supposed they were far beyond the reach of a human voice, was enough to give almost anyone a start.

Yet Tad was not as much surprised as were his companions, for it will be rememberred he already had been through the experience that was so new to the others.

"Who are you?" demanded Mr. Phipps almost sternly.

There was no reply to his question.

"Tad, are you sure that is the same voice?"

"Positive. There can be no doubt. And, besides, she has

used the same words."

"But it's impossible," insisted the young engineer. "No one, let alone a woman, could get near enough to this chamber to be heard as distinctly as that."

"I - I think it must be somebody who can go right through a rock," stammered Ned.

"Ghosts," nodded Walter.

"That's what I thought at first. But I knew it couldn't be after I had time to think twice. And I -"

"He-l-l-l-o-o-o!"

"There it goes again," fairly shouted Tom Phipps. "I'm going to find out what this means before I'm another minute older."

Hastily lighting a match he made a tour of the chamber, every corner of which he examined carefully, ending by a long, critical survey of the hole in the roof.

"It is just as impossible for anyone to be up there as it is to expect to see some one walk through the solid rocks here beside us," he decided, throwing the spent match on the floor where it glowed briefly and went out, leaving the darkness more dense than before.

Tad struck a fresh match.

"Hello, what's this?" he cried, reaching for a small package that lay wrapped in a piece of newspaper on the floor near him. "I didn't see that before."

"Doughnuts!" shouted Ned, who had been peering curiously over Tad's shoulder as the latter opened the package.

"Yes, and they are real," exulted Tad. Already one of them was in his mouth, and the others of the party quickly helped themselves. There was just enough to go around.

"I don't care who you are, but we're much obliged just the same," called Ned in a muffled voice.

"Yes, there's nothing ghostly about this 'bear sign,'" added Tad.

As for their companion, Tom Phipps, words failed him.

"I'm sure I'm going crazy now," he said. "If you are real, for goodness' sake tell us who you are and where you are?" he pleaded.

A merry, chuckling laugh answered him.

"She's up there!" said Tad Butler sharply. He had been listening with every sense on the alert, determined to locate the owner of the voice when next she spoke. Now he was sure that he had succeeded. "I know where you are but I don't know how you ever got there."

"Do you know a way out of this?" interjected Walter.

"Of course," answered the girl.

Tad nodded to his companions. They were burning up their matches very fast now in an effort to catch sight of the owner of the voice.

"How did you suppose I got there if I didn't know the way?"

"No ghost about that, I guess," said the boy.

"Will you help us to get out of here?" asked Tom.

"Can't."

"Why not?" demanded Ned.

"Can you climb up here?"

"No, certainly not."

"Well, that's the answer."

They laughed in spite of themselves.

"Will you tell us how you got where you are?" asked Mr. Phipps.

"That's a secret," replied the girl.

"And I presume your name is a secret too?"

"Yes."

"We'll find out who you are when we get out of here. I promise you that," threatened the assistant superintendent.

"Then good-bye."

"No, no, don't go! Don't go!" begged Tad.

"Say you won't tell on her, Mr. Phipps. "Don't you see -"

"All right, girl, I'll promise to keep your secret."

"You'd better," retorted the girl.

"How did you know we were here?" asked Mr. Phipps.

"I didn't. I heard about the explosion, so I came in here to see if my cave had been harmed any."

"You knew we were right under it, then?"

"Of course. How stupid you are!"

"Where is your cave?"

"I'm in it."

"Yes, I understand that, but where?"

"You ask too many questions."

"Say, young lady, can you find a rope that will reach down to us?" asked Tad, who had been turning over a plan in his mind.

"I guess."

"Please do so then. And hurry, won't you?"

"You will ask no questions?"

"Certainly not!"

"You won't try to find out anything about my cave?"

"No, no, of course not," answered Mr. Phipps impatiently.

"And you will do as I tell you?"

"Yes."

"All right. I'll be back in a minute."

Mr. Phipps sat down nonplussed. "I never was so mixed up in my life," he grumbled. "I can't understand it at all. How did she ever get there?"

"She says it's a cave," suggested Tad.

"But I know of no caves about here."

Tad shrugged his shoulders. That there was one and through it a prospect of their being liberated from their unpleasant and perilous position, was enough for him to know.

"Hello," shouted the girl after a few minutes.

"Yes, did you get the rope?" called Tad excitedly.

"Uh-huh."

"Then drop the end of it down."

A heavy coil hit Tad on the top of his head, nearly knocking him down. He scrambled from under while from above there sounded a peal of merry laughter.

"I don't care, so long as we have the rope," laughed the boy.

"Can you fasten the end of the rope to something up there?"

"No."

"Oh, pshaw! that's too bad," grumbled the boy. "But wait a minute."

Striking a match and shading his eyes with one hand, he peered up to the hole in the rocks. He noted a long narrowing crevice extending back from the main opening.

"I'll tell you what to do."

"Yes."

"Draw the rope into that crack as far as it will go, then tie a knot in the rope so it cannot slip through. I'll climb up -"

"You couldn't get up here. The end of the crack is too far from the place you see. Hold on, here's another crack just like it, right here in the rocks by me. I'll fix it. You all promise not to tell on me?" insisted the girl.

"Yes, yes, yes, we promise. We'll promise anything just now," laughed Ned.

An interval of silence followed while the girl was adjusting the end of the rope. Then she called down to them:

"All ready?" asked Tad.

"Yes, try it."

Tad grasped the rope, and swinging himself clear of the floor, jounced up and down several times.

"I guess it will hold. I'll go up first to see that the rope is secure; then the rest of you can follow me up."

"Why, I couldn't climb that rope to save my life," objected Mr. Phipps.

"I'll fix it so you can. I'll tie some knots in it, then climbing will be easy."

With that Tad once more swung clear of the floor and went up hand over hand with amazing rapidity. By the light of their matches they saw him disappear through the hole in the roof of the chamber.

"It's all right, fellows," he called down to the others. "I'll just haul up the rope and fix it for you."

This he did, letting the rope down to them a few moments later. Walter was the first to try the climb.

"I can't do it, Tad. I just can't," he cried, slipping back to the floor where he landed in a heap.

"Hold the rope down for him, then he ought to be able to make it," directed Tad.

Walter, however, had apparently lost his courage and

declared that he could not do it.

"Take a hitch under his arms, good and strong. I'll pull him up," he commanded. They did as the boy above directed, then Tad began his pull. It was a fearful task.

"Grab hold of me, put your arms around my waist and brace yourself," he commanded, and the girl with quick wit comprehended what he wished her to do. Slowly, foot by foot Tad hauled the dead weight up. The last few feet of the rope seemed a mile to him.

With a final desperate effort, just as his muscles seemed to be at the breaking point, Tad, hauled his companion safely to the flat rock beside him, then fell on the floor of the cave, gasping for breath.

"Le - let the r-rope down," he said faintly.

The girl obeyed.

Ned shinned it with little difficulty, Tom Phipps insisting that the lad should precede him, though Ned wanted him to go first.

Tad was on his feet again.

"Can you make it?" he called down.

"I don't know. I'm going to make a big attempt at it," answered the miner. They heard the rope creak and knew that he had thrown his weight upon it.

"I'm afraid I can't get all the way up. My arms are giving out," they heard him gasp.

"Don't let go! Don't let go!"

"I'm afraid I can't help it, my muscles won't stand the strain."

"Twist the rope about one leg and rest. You can hang there all day if you'll do that," snapped Tad. "How is it!"

"Yes, that works fine. My arms are all a-tremble. I didn't suppose I was so weak?"

"You are not used to it, that's all. That's right; come along. I'll strike a match to light the way."

Little by little and with frequent rests, Tom worked his way up and up until within reach of Tad's strong arm. The lad grasped him by the coat collar and pulled him clear of the hole, dropping him flat on his back safe and sound on the rock where he had previously dumped Walter.

"Good gracious!" breathed Mr. Phipps. "Boy, you must be made of cast iron. You - you pulled me up here with one hand."

"You're here, that's all we need worry about just now," answered Tad, breathing heavily. "Now, Miss, will you please tell us how to get out of here?"

"Come," she said, taking Tad by the hand. She turned away, the others following in single file.

Almost at once they emerged into a high-ceilinged cave, dimly lighted as if through stained glass windows.

The lads uttered an exclamation of amazement.

"I know you now. You're Rose Cravath, Tom Cravath's daughter!" cried Phipps, striding forward and grasping the girl by the shoulder. "I demand to know what all this means?"

Tad stepped between them, pushing Tom aside.

"Remember your promise, Mr. Phipps," he warned.

"Yes, but do you realize where we are, boys?"

"No, and I don't care."

"We're in the Ruby Mountain."

"Look! Look!" shouted Tad excitedly, grasping the arm of Phipps.

With this, he dashed away to a distant part of the chamber that lay in deep gloom. Phipps looked in bewilderment.

A few moments later, Tad emerged from the darkness leading a broncho.

"Didn't I tell you?" he asked triumphantly. "I knew I'd get him some day - this is my stolen broncho." And then patting the pony's neck affectionately, he added: "Good old fellow. I'm glad to have you again."

He had indeed recovered his pony. Probably awaiting the departure of the Pony Riders from Ruby Mountain, the desperadoes had kept the pony - with two others - secreted in the mountain chamber. The other two ponies did not, however, belong to the Pony Rider Boys, much to the disgust of the latter.

"Just Tad's luck," growled Ned.

CHAPTER XXIV

CONCLUSION

Before the Pony Rider Boys had an opportunity to voice their astonishment, Rose held up a hand for silence. Voices were heard approaching.

"Hurry, hurry!" she whispered excitedly, leading the way through a low, narrow opening into another part of the cave.

Tom Phipps's hat was knocked off by the low archway, but not realizing the loss of it, he did not stop. As they entered the second chamber, which was even more brightly lighted than the one they had just left, they heard the sound of water, but were unable to locate the stream which they knew must be near by.

The voices died away to a low murmur and the girl who had been trembling violently, began creeping cautiously toward the opening to reconnoitre when all at once she started back with a little cry of alarm.

Before the eyes of the astonished boys there suddenly appeared two men. Mr. Phipps's hat had warned the men of the presence of strangers in their stronghold. Their faces, therefore, reflected anger instead of surprise.

For a few seconds the newcomers stood glaring at Phipps and the Pony Rider Boys.

"Tom Cravath!" exclaimed the assistant superintendent. "So, you are the mystery, are you?"

"Poaching, eh?" sneered Cravath unabashed.

"What business you got in here?" snapped his companion.

"I might ask you the same question, you fellow and Tom Cravath?" retorted Mr. Phipps, holding the two men with a level gaze. "And what's more I think your peculiar doings will bear looking into. There's something mighty queer about this business. I shouldn't be surprised if we found we'd solved a greater mystery than we thought -"

"You'll solve nothing!" shouted Cravath, suddenly drawing a revolver. His companion did likewise, both men quickly covering Tom Phipps and the boys with their weapons. "You'll find it ain't profitable to meddle with other folks' business."

"Pity you hadn't learned that lesson yourself," jeered Tom.

"It's over the cliff for the whole blooming bunch of you. I'll give you all the mystery you want."

"Father, father," protested Rose, horrified at her parent's cold-blooded threat. "They haven't done anything. They -"

"You shut up!" roared the miner. "Get out of here! Get

in under the arch there! I'll attend to you later!"

The girl hesitated, then crept away sobbing as Cravath made a threatening move toward her.

"Now, I'll settle with you and your bunch of meddling tenderfeet," announced Cravath sternly. "Right about face!"

They hesitated, then turned in obedience to his command. There seemed nothing else for them to do, for both men were fingering their weapons suggestively.

"These boys have done nothing to harm you, Cravath," protested Mr. Phipps. "And no more have I. Mark me, you'll pay for this indignity, and dearly too."

"You don't say?" sneered the miner.

"I suppose this is where you hide the ponies you have been stealing," said Phipps boldly, a sudden thought having come to him.

"Forward march!" roared the enraged miner.

"Not - not over the cliff - you - you can't mean it?" begged Phipps, his face going suddenly pale.

"That's what I mean. You fellows are supposed to be buried in the mine down there. It'll take 'em months to blast into the place where they think you are, and when they reach the place you all will be gone a long time."

Cravath laughed harshly.

"Come now, over you go, unless you prefer to stand there and take your medicine."

"Hold on there a minute. I guess if anybody does the leap for life, it'll be you that does it," shouted a voice behind the two desperate men.

A second dynamite explosion could not have surprised them more. The men wheeled like a flash.

From the shadow of the archway, through which they had just entered, protruded a rifle barrel. The Pony Rider Boys who had also turned sharply at the interruption, observed that the gun barrel had a telescope attachment. Their eyes following further back, observed something else, too.

"Chunky!" gasped the lads in one voice.

Cravath made a move to level his weapon at the boy who had interfered with his plans thus unexpectedly.

"You stop that, now! I've got six bullets in this gun. If you get me excited I may press too hard on the trigger, and - well, maybe you'll think you've stepped into a hornets' nest. Drop those pistols!"

The muzzle of the repeating rifle never wavered. Behind the sights, the eyes of Stacy Brown had contracted into two narrow slits.

The desperadoes hesitated, measuring their chances shrewdly. They must have considered that these were not worth the taking, for they permitted their fingers to relax, the weapons falling to the floor with a clatter.

Chunky lowered his rifle ever so little, and the Pony Riders uttered a yell of triumph.

For one brief instant Chunky was off his guard. In that second he lost his prisoners.

With a bound the two men cleared the intervening space that lay between them and the cliff. They reached it at a point near the corner of the chamber some distance from where they had attempted to drive the boys over. Throwing themselves flat on their faces, they wriggled over the edge and disappeared. A faint splash below, a few seconds later, told the lads that their desperate assailants had reached the water.

"They'll drown, they'll drown!" cried Walter.

"No such luck," growled Tom Phipps. "They've got away, that's all. They know what they're doing."

Chunky swaggered to the edge with rifle dropped over his left arm, and peered over.

"Guess I'll hurry 'em along," he announced, clearing his weapon for action.

Tad sprang forward and forced the barrel up.

"Chunky, Chunky!" he warned.

"I was just going to scare 'em, that's all," grinned the fat boy, lowering his rifle.

At that moment the boys fell upon Chunky, fairly hugging him in their delight. After the keen edge of their excitement had worn off, they pressed him for the story of how he had happened to find his way into the Ruby Mountain at that time.

The lad explained that having been hunting in that vicinity and becoming tired out he had sat down to rest. While thus engaged the men had come along. They were talking of the explosion, and from them he learned that the drift in which the Pony Rider Boys were imprisoned was immediately beneath their hiding place in the Ruby Mountain.

Interested at once, the lad followed them into the mountain.

"But, how did they get in here?" demanded Tom.

"Through a hole in the rocks, that went straight in."

Phipps insisted on being taken to the place at once. He found that entrance had been made through an abandoned shaft that extended into the mountain a short distance on the level. A door had been skilfully constructed, shutting off the entrance to the cave itself. Years before a notorious band of outlaws had been known to have a hiding place somewhere in the vicinity. Tom Cravath and his associates had come upon it and used it for their own nefarious purposes.

"I think we'll find we've come upon a very important discovery," decided Mr. Phipps after listening to the fat boy's story. And so it proved.

Cravath had been at the head of a band of thieves, who made way with their plunder through the Ruby Mountain. A large quantity of it was found there on the following day. As for the stock which they stole, this was led into the mine entrance, down into a subterranean water course along which it was directed for several miles along towards the Indian Territory where it was eventually sold by other members of the gang.

No trace of any of the desperate band was ever found. Eagle-eye, the missing Indian guide, was discovered bound and gagged in a remote chamber in the Ruby Mountain, weak from loss of food. He had caught some of the band stealing the ponies and they had taken him prisoner.

It was proved, however, that neither Rose Cravath nor her mother had any knowledge of the transactions of the desperate band.

Great was the rejoicing in the mining camp when the news of the discovery became noised about. The lads were made heroes by the enthusiastic miners. But this did not bring back the lost ponies. Rather than purchase others for the brief time they would be in the Ozarks, it was decided to close the trip and continue their journeyings amidst other scenes.

On the second morning after their exciting experiences in the mines they rode away, bound for the nearest railroad station, all anticipation at the prospect of a sojourn on the great Nevada desert, of which they had heard so much. How they lost themselves there, their efforts to extricate themselves from the desert maze, attended by a remarkable series of strange happenings, will be told in a following volume entitled, "THE PONY RIDER BOYS IN THE ALKALI."

Choose from Thousands of 1stWorldLibrary Classics By

Adolphus WilliamWard
Aesop
Agatha Christie
Alexander Aaronsohn
Alexander Kielland
Alexandre Dumas
Alfred Gatty
Alfred Ollivant
Alice Duer Miller
Alice Turner Curtis
Alice Dunbar
Ambrose Bierce
Amelia E. Barr
Andrew Lang
Andrew McFarland Davis
Anna Sewell
Annie Besant
Annie Hamilton Donnell
Annie Payson Call
Anton Chekhov
Arnold Bennett
Arthur Conan Doyle
Arthur Ransome
Atticus
B. M. Bower
Basil King
Bayard Taylor
Ben Macomber
Booth Tarkington
Bram Stoker
C. Collodi
C. E. Orr
C. M. Ingleby
Carolyn Wells
Catherine Parr Traill
Charles A. Eastman
Charles Dickens
Charles Dudley Warner
Charles Farrar Browne
Charles Ives
Charles Kingsley
Charles Lathrop Pack
Charles Whibley
Charles Willing Beale
Charlotte M. Braeme
Charlotte M.Yonge
Clair W. Hayes
Clarence Day Jr.
Clarence E. Mulford
Clemence Housman
Confucius
Cornelis DeWitt Wilcox
Cyril Burleigh
D. H. Lawrence
Daniel Defoe
David Garnett
Don Carlos Janes
Donald Keyhole
Dorothy Kilner
Dougan Clark
E. Nesbit
E.P.Roe
E. Phillips Oppenheim
Edgar Allan Poe
Edgar Rice Burroughs
Edith Wharton
Edward J. O'Biren
John Cournos
Edwin L. Arnold
Eleanor Atkins
Elizabeth Cleghorn
Gaskell
Elizabeth Von Arnim
Ellem Key
Emily Dickinson
Erasmus W. Jones
Ernie Howard Pie
Ethel Turner
Ethel Watts Mumford
Eugenie Foa
Eugene Wood
Evelyn Everett-Green
Everard Cotes
F. J. Cross
Federick Austin Ogg
Ferdinand Ossendowski
Francis Bacon
Francis Darwin
Frances Hodgson Burnett
Frank Gee Patchin
Frank Harris
Frank Jewett Mather
Frank L. Packard
Frederick Trevor Hill
Frederick Winslow Taylor
Friedrich Kerst
Friedrich Nietzsche
Fyodor Dostoyevsky
Gabrielle E. Jackson
Garrett P. Serviss
Gaston Leroux
George Ade
Geroge Bernard Shaw
George Ebers
George Eliot
George MacDonald
George Orwell
George Tucker
George W. Cable
George Wharton James
Gertrude Atherton
Grace E. King
Grant Allen
Guillermo A. Sherwell
Gulielma Zollinger
Gustav Flaubert
H. A. Cody
H. B. Irving
H. G. Wells
H. H. Munro
H. Irving Hancock
H. Rider Haggard
H. W. C. Davis
Hamilton Wright Mabie
Hans Christian Andersen
Harold Avery
Harold McGrath
Harriet Beecher Stowe
Harry Houidini
Helent Hunt Jackson
Helen Nicolay
Hendy David Thoreau
Henrik Ibsen
Henry Adams
Henry Ford
Henry Frost
Henry James
Henry Jones Ford
Henry Seton Merriman
Henry Wadsworth
Longfellow
Henry W Longfellow
Herbert A. Giles
Herbert N. Casson
Herman Hesse
Homer
Honore De Balzac

Horace Walpole
Horatio Alger, Jr.
Howard Pyle
Howard R. Garis
Hugh Lofting
Hugh Walpole
Humphry Ward
Ian Maclaren
Israel Abrahams
J.G.Austin
J. Henri Fabre
J. M. Barrie
J. Macdonald Oxley
J. S. Knowles
J. Storer Clouston
Jack London
Jacob Abbott
James Allen
James Lane Allen
James Andrews
James Baldwin
James DeMille
James Joyce
James Oliver Curwood
James Oppenheim
James Otis
Jane Austen
Jens Peter Jacobsen
Jerome K. Jerome
John Burroughs
John F. Kennedy
John Gay
John Glasworthy
John Habberton
John Joy Bell
John Milton
John Philip Sousa
Jonathan Swift
Joseph Carey
Joseph Conrad
Joseph Jacobs
Julian Hawthrone
Julies Vernes
Justin Huntly McCarthy
Kakuzo Okakura
Kenneth Grahame
Kate Langley Bosher
L. A. Abbot
L. T. Meade
L. Frank Baum
Laura Lee Hope
Laurence Housman
Leo Tolstoy
Leonid Andreyev
Lewis Carroll
Lilian Bell
Lloyd Osbourne
Louis Tracy
Louisa May Alcott
Lucy Fitch Perkins
Lucy Maud Montgomery
Lydia Miller Middleton
Lyndon Orr
M. H. Adams
Margaret E. Sangster
Margaret Vandercook
Maria Edgeworth
Maria Thompson Daviess
Mariano Azuela
Marion Polk Angellotti
Mark Overton
Mark Twain
Mary Austin
Mary Cole
Mary Rowlandson
Mary Wollstonecraft
Shelley
Max Beerbohm
Myra Kelly
Nathaniel Hawthrone
O. F. Walton
Oscar Wilde
Owen Johnson
P.G.Wodehouse
Paul and Mable Thorn
Paul G. Tomlinson
Paul Severing
Peter B. Kyne
Plato
R. Derby Holmes
R. L. Stevenson
Rabindranath Tagore
Rahul Alvares
Ralph Waldo Emmerson
Rene Descartes
Rex E. Beach
Richard Harding Davis
Richard Jefferies
Robert Barr
Robert Frost
Robert Gordon Anderson
Robert L. Drake
Robert Lansing
Robert Michael Ballantyne
Robert W. Chambers
Rosa Nouchette Carey
Ross Kay
Rudyard Kipling
Samuel B. Allison
Samuel Hopkins Adams
Sarah Bernhardt
Selma Lagerlof
Sherwood Anderson
Sigmund Freud
Standish O'Grady
Stanley Weyman
Stella Benson
Stephen Crane
Stewart Edward White
Stijn Streuvels
Swami Abhedananda
Swami Parmananda
T. S. Ackland
The Princess Der Ling
Thomas A. Janvier
Thomas A Kempis
Thomas Anderton
Thomas Bailey Aldrich
Thomas Bulfinch
Thomas De Quincey
Thomas H. Huxley
Thomas Hardy
Thomas More
Thornton W. Burgess
U. S. Grant
Valentine Williams
Victor Appleton
Virginia Woolf
Walter Scott
Washington Irving
Wilbur Lawton
Wilkie Collins
Willa Cather
Willard F. Baker
William Makepeace
Thackeray
William W. Walter
Winston Churchill
Yei Theodora Ozaki
Young E. Allison
Zane Grey

www.ingramcontent.com/pod-product-compliance
Lightning Source LLC
LaVergne TN
LVHW090600110826
845146LV00001B/199